Shifting
Sands

Shifting Sands

LIFE IN THE TIMES OF MOSES, JESUS, AND MUHAMMAD

By KATHY LOWINGER

annick press
toronto + new york + vancouver

Edited by Catherine Marjoribanks
Designed by Kong Njo

Annick Press Ltd.

We acknowledge the support of the Canada Council for the Arts, the Ontario Arts Council, and the Government of Canada through the Canada Book Fund (CBF) for our publishing activities.

Cataloging in Publication

Lowinger, Kathy, author
     Shifting sands : life in the times of Moses, Jesus, and Muhammad / Kathy Lowinger.

ISBN 978-1-55451-617-9 (bound). – ISBN 978-1-55451-616-2 (pbk.)

     I. Title.

PS8623.O8885S55 2014   jC813'.6   C2013-906980-1

Distributed in Canada by:	Published in the U.S.A. by:
Firefly Books Ltd.	Annick Press (U.S.) Ltd.
50 Staples Avenue, Unit 1	Distributed in the U.S.A. by:
Richmond Hill, ON	Firefly Books (U.S.) Inc.
L4B 1H1	P.O. Box 1338, Ellicott Station
	Buffalo, NY 14205

Printed in Canada

Visit us at: www.annickpress.com
Visit Wylie Beckert at: www.wyliebeckert.com

Also available in e-book format. Please visit www.annickpress.com/ebooks.html for more details. Or scan

FOR BILL HARNUM

EGYPT IN THE TIME OF MOSES

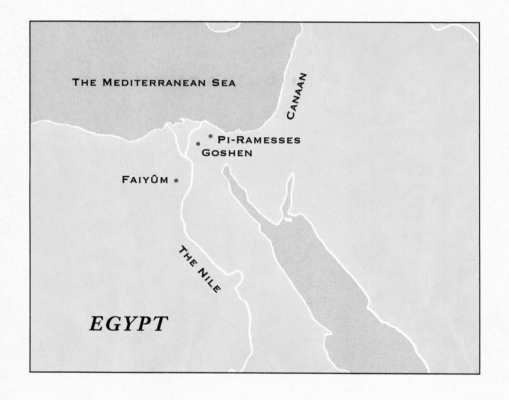

THE ROMAN EMPIRE IN THE TIME OF JESUS

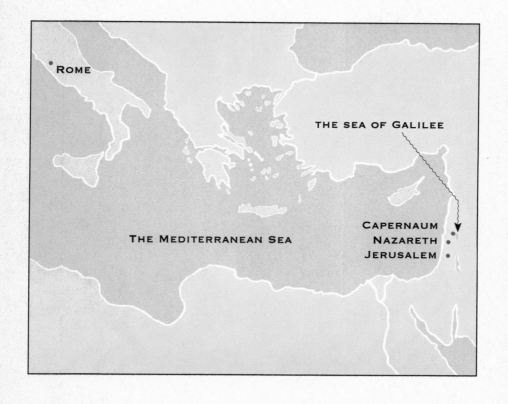

ROME

THE SEA OF GALILEE

THE MEDITERRANEAN SEA

CAPERNAUM
NAZARETH
JERUSALEM

ARABIA IN THE TIME OF MUHAMMAD

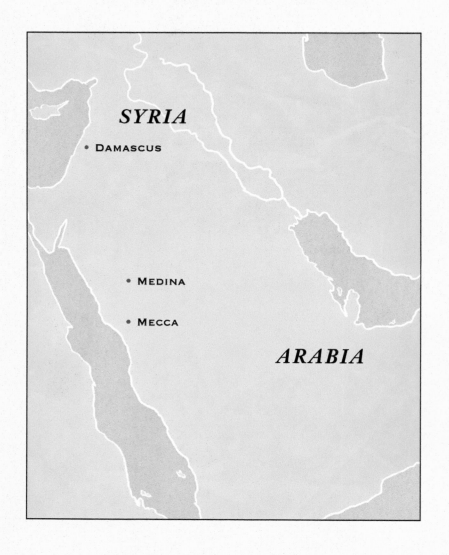

AUTHOR'S NOTE

I haven't set out to write a history of three of the most important people who have ever lived. Many wise scholars have filled whole buildings with such books. And I haven't set out to describe or to compare Judaism, Christianity, and Islam. Again, many people who are much more qualified than I am have done that. It's possible to spend years studying Moses, Jesus, or Muhammad, and if you're interested in learning more, you'll find all kinds of fascinating and inspiring information.

I've written a work of fiction. I've shifted events and sometimes I've combined them, I've created characters, and I've made up what people said. But all along, I've tried to imagine what it must have been like to live in the time and place where Moses, or Jesus, or Muhammad lived. I hope I've been able to capture the spirit of those long-ago times that continue to shape our lives.

DINA

The doorkeeper of the House of Weavers thumped the floor with his heavy wooden staff. "Slaves, cease your clatter!"

We stopped our work at the looms and flexed our stiff fingers. He stepped aside to make way for an attendant of the Mistress of the House of Weavers.

The attendant held up a piece of woven white linen. I recognized the delicate pattern right away.

"Who is the weaver responsible for this?" demanded the attendant.

I raised my hand. I was proud of my work. Though I was only fourteen, I was already a skillful weaver. "I did it."

The attendant barked, "Then you are to follow me! The Queen wishes to see you."

I felt my face turn red. The Pharaoh had one hundred wives, each of whom had a special duty to perform for his household, but the only one I had ever seen was the Mistress of the House of Weavers. And she summoned her slaves only when she wanted to punish them, usually with a whipping. She was fond of saying, "A slave's ear is on her back! That is the only way she can listen." Had I done something wrong? Or perhaps one of the other slaves was jealous of how well I could weave and had spread false tales about me. That would not have been surprising.

I had been squatting on my work stool for hours, so my legs almost buckled when I got to my feet. Ora, the slave who sometimes shared my loom, mouthed the word "Courage" to me as I followed the attendant into the sunshine. I stumbled, blinded by the sun after the gloom inside the House of Weavers.

I hurried after the attendant, too nervous to notice much, but I had a fleeting impression of the huge buildings, their graceful balconies decorated with bright blue tiles, the heat that shimmered around the glass and bronze workshops, the sound of horses whinnying in their stables. Beyond the walls that surrounded the palace grounds I could hear loud hammering. *Maybe my father is lifting one of those hammers*, I thought. He was a slave, like me, a foreman doing the brutal and dangerous work of building the Pharaoh's grand new city, Pi-Ramesses. *Father, I wish you were here to help me now!*

Finally we got to the glorious, luxurious palace that housed all the queens. A guard searched me, then pointed to a stone basin. "Wash yourself," he ordered. My hands shook as I splashed perfumed water on my feet.

The royal chamber was dazzling. The walls were painted with pictures of the many gods and goddesses that the Egyptians worshipped, separated by brilliant bands of red and yellow. The Egyptians worshipped different gods who could help with different things: a god for war and battle, a goddess for music and dance, a god for writing and knowledge. Some of them looked like men and women, some like birds and animals—a jackal, a hawk, a cat—and some had the heads of birds and animals but the bodies of people. The Pharaoh himself was not just a king—he was a god too. It was all a jumble to me.

As I knelt before the Queen, I prayed, but not to any of these gods. I was a Hebrew. For generations, my people had believed in only one God, an all-powerful God, the God of everything.

The Queen was seated on a gilded wooden chair, and I could smell the sweet ointments that had been rubbed into her skin. Her eyes were rimmed with a sweep of black kohl that made them look like the eyes of a cat—just like the gray cat that was curled on her lap.

As I knelt before her, I kept my eyes fixed on the painting on the floor in front of me: a hunter and his dog chasing a deer. I braced myself for a beating.

Instead, the Queen spoke. "I have a gift for you."

At first my frightened mind garbled her words; I couldn't believe I had heard her correctly. Then the attendant prodded me with her toe. "You have pleased the Queen with your work," she whispered.

I dared to look up.

"Your weaving is skillful." I felt so relieved that I wanted to cry, but the Queen was speaking again. "I have decided to reward you."

The cat jumped to the floor and the Queen tugged on the leash attached to its jeweled collar.

I held my breath. The Queen motioned to a chest covered in gold. An attendant brought out a pair of delicately carved leather sandals. Even the soles were carved with an intricate design. She placed them on the floor in front of me. Because a royal person could not wear anything that was stained or torn, damaged items were often passed on to servants, and sometimes even to slaves. The toe loop on one of these sandals had come loose—but I didn't care. I had never owned anything so lovely.

I hugged them to my chest. This was a great honor. The other weavers certainly had reason to be jealous now!

I started to thank the Queen, but she raised her hand. "There is something more. After the coming Festival, I am moving my court south to the Faiyûm Oasis, and I am choosing the slaves who will come with me. You have pleased me, so you are to be one of them."

The Faiyûm Oasis. The words sounded wonderfully lush to me. I had heard stories about Faiyûm's trees heavy with fruit, its streams of clear, cool water, and its famous sacred crocodiles, fed with cakes. I was thrilled to be one of the chosen.

Only one shadow fell over my happiness, and that was the thought of leaving my family even farther behind. My people lived in a village in Goshen. I had not been back there since I had left it seven years earlier, but still, it was comforting to know that it was only a day's walk away. Once I was in Faiyûm, would the court stay there? Would I ever see my home again, my father, my grandfather? I was almost glad that I had no choice in the matter.

"Eleven, twelve, thirteen, fourteen . . ." The doorkeeper counted us as we lined up for our meal. I took my bread and bowl of stewed vegetables to the corner of the House of Weavers where Ora was sitting. We'd been friends since the day Ora had arrived, snarling like a cornered dog. She wasn't a Hebrew slave from Goshen; she had been captured in a war in far-off Nubia, in the south. Shackled with wooden manacles on their wrists and ropes around their necks, her whole family had been marched to Egypt to work as slaves. Ora was the only one who had survived.

She asked, "Did the Queen order you to be beaten? Dina, are you all right?"

"I'm fine. Nobody touched me. Ora, you won't believe this. I can barely believe it myself. The Queen gave me a pair of her own sandals, and told me I would go with her court to Faiyûm."

Ora snorted. "Oh, I see. So . . . how does it feel to be one of her pets?"

I didn't want to argue with her. Ora had learned to be a good weaver, but she would never forget how she had been torn away from her homeland, her people, her tribe, and forced into slavery. She would never be able to return to her own home. Anger flowed in her like blood.

I suppose it was different for me. I knew I was a slave, but still, I had food, a place to sleep, and now I even had the Queen's favor. Though I would never have admitted it to Ora, I thought that life in the House of Weavers, even though we were always at the mercy of our Egyptian masters, might be the best life for me.

When nighttime came, we all unrolled our sleeping mats on the stone floor of the storehouse next to the weavers' building. I laid my head on the Queen's sandals and listened to the sleep sounds of the other slaves. When I finally fell asleep too, I dreamed I was home in Goshen.

Goshen was the part of Egypt where the Hebrews lived— at least, those who weren't slaves in the Pharaoh's court or constructing Pi-Ramesses, the magnificent city the Pharaoh was building to remind the people that he was no mere man but a god. Many women and children and a handful of old people had remained in Goshen, tending flocks of sheep and goats. That was not to be my fate. I didn't remember my mother, but all my life I'd heard about what a fine weaver she had been. Before she died, she had arranged for me to become a weaver too, and to take her place just as soon as I was old enough. I would be a slave in the House of Weavers, just like her.

In my dream, it was the night before I left my village for Pi-Ramesses. I was seven years old again, sitting with my grandfather by the fire, listening to the women sing their songs in praise of the new moon.

To my surprise, my grandfather dabbed his eyes with his sleeve.

"What's wrong, Grandfather?"

"Tomorrow you will go to Pi-Ramesses to the House of Weavers. I am afraid that I will lose you. We've been lucky to have you this long, but you're a big girl now."

One of the women overheard. "There's no reason to cry, old man. Her lot will be easier than ours. She will have food and drink, and a dry place to sleep. Her mother, God rest her soul, was a weaver once. This is what she would have wanted for Dina."

Grandfather clasped my face between his rough hands. "You will see many wondrous things, child. You will see golden statues of gods everywhere. The Egyptians' ways will tempt you. Promise me that you will not forget who you are. You are a Hebrew, part of a proud people. We were not always slaves, and the day will come again when we will be free to worship God. Ours is the God of everything. Never forget that. Do not forget who you are!"

His words were ringing in my ears when I woke up. The Queen's sandals had left a mark on my cheek.

The Pharaoh's servants picked their way around our looms, handing out a portion of beer and two small loaves of bread to each of us. Every day hundreds of loaves were baked for Pharaoh. Leftovers were given out around the court. Many of the girls devoured theirs on the spot, but though I was hungry, I put my loaves aside. They would come in handy.

By noon, the dusty air inside the windowless House of Weavers was so hot that we couldn't work. We were allowed a few minutes of rest in the shady courtyard, under the doorkeeper's sullen gaze. That day I signaled to the doorkeeper. When I was sure he was watching, I put one of my loaves of bread in a niche in the wall. The doorkeeper must have been pleased with the bribe, because he looked away as I slipped out of the courtyard with the other loaf of bread. I ran through the palace grounds, empty in the baking heat.

I found my father directing a line of slaves who were building a wall. I knew there was only time for a few words—one loaf of bread wasn't going to buy more than a few minutes of the doorkeeper's mercy—but I had to tell Father about Faiyûm.

When he saw me crossing toward him, he looked around nervously. "Dina, I'm happy to see you, but you know you're not supposed to be here. If you're discovered, they'll show no mercy."

"Don't worry, Father. Look, I've brought you bread. And I have wonderful news—that's why I've come. The Queen has praised my weaving. She thinks I am talented, and she has chosen me to move to Faiyûm with her. Me!"

"Faiyûm! I have heard stories from other slaves, the lucky ones who traveled there with the Pharaoh's court. They say the oasis is full of marvels, like nothing you've ever seen before in your life. But when will we be together again? I will miss you, Daughter."

"I thought you'd be pleased for me, Father."

"I am. I am. I'm proud that you are such a good weaver."

Before he could say more, a Hebrew slave, faint from the scorching sun, called out, "Please, may I have a sip of water?" Father signaled for the others to pause so that the slave could take a drink.

The Egyptian overseer had been some distance away, sheltering from the noonday sun in one of the few slivers of shade on the building site, but now they heard him shout, "Lazy, worthless dog!" He came running, and brought his heavy club down on the poor wretch's head. My father tried to help, but it was too late. The Hebrew slave, crumpled in the dust, was already dead.

"Whoever dares to object will be next!" the overseer announced. Then he turned his wrath on my father. "One less slave on your crew! Don't use that as an excuse to fall behind in your work or you too will feel the weight of my club—or worse!"

I wanted to scream and curse, but Father dug his fingers into my arm. In Hebrew he said to me, "I am no Moses. And fighting with the overseer cannot help this poor man anymore. Now go! Go quickly, before the overseer asks questions."

I fled.

"I am no Moses," my father had said. Moses was a Hebrew who had stood up to the Egyptians to defend a slave.

Moses had been born at a terrible time. The old pharaoh was afraid there were too many Hebrews in Egypt, and that they might become powerful, so he ordered that every Hebrew male baby be killed. Moses' mother and his sister Miriam, who lived in our village, were desperate. They devised a clever plan to save him by hiding him among the reeds on the banks of the river Nile, hoping to fetch him after the brutal order had been carried out.

The Pharaoh's daughter, who had gone down to the river to wash, found the baby. Miriam had been hiding in the reeds, keeping watch over her tiny brother. When she saw that the Pharaoh's daughter had taken pity on the helpless baby, she did something very brave: she approached the princess. She told her that she knew of a Hebrew woman—her own mother, of course—who would make a fine nurse for the baby. So Moses' mother was able to take care of her boy until he was old enough to go to the palace, where the princess raised him as her own.

At court, Moses was not a slave like me. He grew up as an equal among the other children, who became his schoolmates, and the Pharaoh's son, Ramses, was his good friend. Then one day a story made its way back to our village with an old man, a slave who had been allowed to return home to die. He told the villagers that Moses, by then grown up, had seen an Egyptian beating a Hebrew slave. Moses had come to the slave's defense and killed the Egyptian overseer. After that, he was branded a dangerous rebel—he had killed one of Pharaoh's servants who had merely been trying to carry out Pharaoh's orders. Moses fled—he had no choice—and nobody had seen him since. But all of this had happened a very long time ago.

My grandfather never forgot that story, and he told it to my father, who told it to me.

Prince Ramses, who had been Moses' friend, was now the Pharaoh of all Egypt. I wondered what had happened to the rebel Moses.

For weeks, golden statues of all the gods were being gathered from all over Egypt for the Sed Festival. It was supposed to celebrate a pharaoh's thirtieth year of power, but most of them didn't wait that long. They held it when they wanted to show that they were still fit to rule. The rituals could last for months. The statues of gods would be set up in their shrines after a torchlight parade and the Pharaoh would make offerings to each one of them. There would be all kinds of festivities: archers would fire arrows into the sky, flocks of birds would be released into the air, and cattle would be driven around the city four times. There would be thrilling athletic contests acting out battles from ancient wars. After the offerings, there was an important ritual that he had to perform by himself. Markers would be set up in a large open space to create a route, and then, with everyone watching, the Pharaoh would have to run between the markers to prove how physically strong and powerful he was. That was the most exciting part. Even slaves would be allowed to watch.

"Won't it be wonderful?" Ora loved the colorful festivals as much as I did. "We'll be given cakes to eat. Best of all, we will have no work for a week. A whole week! We can spend it together!"

Her words gave me an idea. A week was enough time for me to go to Goshen and back. Everyone would be caught up in the rituals, so they wouldn't miss me, and I would be back before it was over. Besides, I had never liked pretending to pray to all the Egyptian gods. Though I didn't want to miss all the sights, the dream I'd had of my grandfather was lingering in my heart. I wanted to see him again, and this would be my best chance—I had to grab it. No weaver had ever been allowed to leave for such a long time, but I was the Queen's favorite. That gave me hope.

"I am not going to the Festival. I'm going to ask the Queen if I can go back to Goshen instead."

"Are you crazy? You can't just talk to royalty. Besides, you're a slave. They'll think you're running away."

"They know I'll come back. Who wouldn't want to go to Faiyûm?"

The royal family were to have new clothes for the rituals, so for the next few days our looms clacked ceaselessly. One morning the Queen came to inspect our work. She walked among the weavers, her tiny red pet monkey perched on her shoulder. Suddenly the monkey leapt to the ground, and it darted under my loom. The Queen screamed. Just as the little animal was about to be crushed by one of the heavy weights, I managed to grab it by the tail.

The Queen smiled and took the creature from my arms. "I see that, once again, I have reason to praise you." This was it! Surely she wouldn't refuse my request now. But before I could say a word, the Queen had moved on. Tears pricked my eyes.

My only other hope was convincing the doorkeeper to let me sneak out. But I'd need more than a loaf of bread to bribe him this time.

During the afternoon break, I found him sprawled under an awning, teasing his pet mouse with a stick. He looked up, his moist lower lip hanging open. I tried not to stare at it. I had rehearsed my speech: "The Queen, in her graciousness, has shown me great kindness. May I take Festival cakes to my old grandfather in Goshen so that he can know of her bounty?"

"Has the sun cooked your brain, girl? Why in the world would I let a slave go so far away?"

"I am among the ones chosen to go to Faiyûm. Of course I will return."

That seemed to make sense to the doorkeeper. He grunted as he got to his feet.

"Every favor has its price. What price are you willing to pay?" He wound a curl of my hair around his grubby finger. I willed myself not to pull away.

"A pair of the queen's sandals."

He threw his head back and laughed. "Do you think I'm stupid? If someone saw me with these, they'd assume I stole them! Are you *trying* to get me killed?" He made a big show of scratching his sweaty shaven head. "Now . . . what other favors can you offer?"

I backed away as quickly as I could.

I hadn't told anyone about my plan to bribe the doorkeeper, because if things went wrong I didn't want any of the other slaves to be whipped for not reporting me. But when Ora found me crying at my loom, she pestered me until I told her what had happened.

When I finished, Ora said, "I have an idea." She sounded very pleased with herself.

I tried to protest. "Please don't get involved. I don't want to get you into trouble. It was foolish of me to think I could go home again. If I'm caught . . ." I didn't even want to think about what might happen to me. "But I want to go home again so badly!"

"Don't give up! If I still had a family of my own to be with, I'd probably try to sneak out too. But don't worry, my plan is going to work. You'll be able to get away, and that toad of a doorkeeper will have to keep his mouth shut, or it might cost him his life." The thought made her cackle.

We put Ora's plan into action. The next day we saved our daily portion of beer and left the flasks where the doorkeeper was sure to find them. Just as she'd predicted, he drank his own and then helped himself to both of ours. Soon he was in a drunken sleep.

I ran past him and all the way to the gates of the palace grounds. As I had hoped, the guards there were busy directing the crowds gathering for the Festival. It was easy to sneak past them.

The sun was low and I had walked many hours when, tired and hungry, I finally came to my own home. Though the tents were shabby, the smell of food cooking and the bleating of the goats and sheep and the sound of people laughing as they went about their work was so comforting and wonderful to me that I almost felt like crying.

I wondered if anyone would recognize me. After all, I had been gone for seven whole years—half my life. The women were gathered at the well, drawing water for the evening meal. One of them looked up and saw me. She cried out, "Why, that girl looks just like Sheva, of beloved memory. It must be Dina, her daughter!"

The next thing I knew, I was being hugged and kissed by chattering, crying women. They clamored to hear news of their husbands and brothers and sons who were working on Pi-Ramesses. Finally, an old woman held up her hand.

"Let the girl catch her breath. First she must be taken to her grandfather. I am Miriam, but I don't suppose you remember me," she said. She led the way toward the village tents, and as she did, she sang all the way.

I felt lightheaded as I walked along the rocky path, strewn with sheep and goat dung. My feet had grown soft walking on the tiled floors of the Pharaoh's court. My plain white tunic, which all the female slaves wore, was out of place amid the Hebrew women's brightly striped woolen clothes. I had forgotten the smell and the dust. In the palace grounds, waving palm fronds wafted perfumes to scent the air, and sometimes the Egyptians even put mounds of wax on their heads that released perfume as it melted. I had grown used to the Egyptians' shaven heads and faces and bodies. The Hebrew men who met us had long hair, heavy beards, and hairy arms.

I recognized our tent. I called out, "Grandfather, I have come home."

A wrinkled hand pushed aside the goatskin that covered the door. Grandfather was more stooped than when I had left, and his hair was whiter, but when he held out his arms, I felt as if no time had passed.

"My child, my child! How is it that you are here? Have you done something wrong? Did you run away? Has something happened to your father?"

"Please don't worry. Father is well, though the work is very hard. As for me, the Queen is so pleased with me that she has chosen me to go with her to the Faiyûm Oasis. I've come to say goodbye and to ask you for your blessing."

He hesitated, taking it all in, and then said, "I am an old man, Granddaughter. If you go far away, I may not live to see you again!" I was afraid he was going to cry, and I felt awful.

"But I'm here now. I wanted you to know that all is well with me. You and Father did right to send me to the House of Weavers."

Someone else now emerged from Grandfather's tent. I hadn't realized he had a guest.

Miriam looked fondly at the stranger. "This is a day of returning, Dina. My brother has come home too. This is my brother, Moses."

I peered at the stranger. Was this bearded man who looked like a common shepherd the Moses my father had told me about, the Moses who had saved a Hebrew slave's life?

Moses turned to go. Grandfather said to him, "Won't you come back later, once I've had a chance to welcome my dear child home? I am eager to hear more about why you've returned."

"Of course." Moses clasped Grandfather's arm and wished us both well.

Grandfather ushered me into the tent, and after I'd eaten a bowl of stewed lentils, I wanted to tell him everything that had happened to me since I'd left Goshen, but I couldn't stop yawning.

Grandfather said, "Dina, we will speak tomorrow. Even with these dim eyes of mine, I can tell you are tired." I didn't protest.

Miriam returned and unrolled a mat for me to sleep on in a corner of the tent. She pulled a woolen cloak over me. It smelled of wet sheep. Moses had come back with her, and after she left, he and Grandfather sat down together by the light of an oil lamp.

I was too exhausted to sleep, so I watched the flickering lamplight and listened to the men. Moses spoke with difficulty, as if there was something wrong with his tongue. He was telling Grandfather that after he'd killed the Egyptian slave driver, he had escaped to the faraway land of Midian, where he had become a shepherd.

I propped myself up on my elbow. "I live in the Pharaoh's court, and I've even been in the Queen's chamber," I said. "Didn't you mind being a shepherd after living in the palace?"

"Shush, Dina!" said Grandfather, but Moses answered.

"Not at all. In Midian I married the high priest's daughter, and we had a son. I grew to love the quiet way of life. I was happy there."

"Then why have you come back?"

This time Grandfather sounded cross. "Dina, Moses is our guest!"

"I had no choice." Moses spoke slowly, as if surprised by his own words. "One day I was out by myself, tending the flock. Suddenly, from a perfectly ordinary bush, flames leapt up. But though the bush crackled and blazed, it didn't burn. At first I thought it was a mirage. Sometimes the desert sun can play tricks on you, you know.

"I stepped closer. Then, out of the roar of the fire, words formed. At first I thought I was hearing my father's gruff voice telling me to take off my sandals because I was standing on holy ground. As I was unlacing them, a voice called out. 'Moses, Moses!' And then I knew: this was the voice of God.

"You can tell that speaking is an ordeal for me, but in spite of my poor scarred tongue, my voice was firm. I answered, 'Here am I.'"

"What an honor!" Grandfather was awed.

"Not one I sought, I assure you. God told me to return to Egypt. I was to tell Pharaoh that he must release the Hebrews from bondage, so that we can live in the land He promised to us so long ago, and we can worship Him freely.

"I thought God was asking too much of me. I knew that I would have to talk to our own elders first, and convince them that I was bringing God's message. I argued that they wouldn't listen to me, that they wouldn't believe me. I've been away so long that they would think of me as a stranger, a fugitive. Besides, you have heard how difficult it is to understand my speech. But it was no use. I had to accept the fact that I was the one who had to ask Pharaoh to release my people."

I listened to the murmur of the men's voices until dawn, when I finally fell asleep.

The sun was already hot when I woke and put on the scratchy woolen tunic Miriam had brought me. Grandfather and I went into the hills to care for the sheep and goats. I had spent the last seven years hemmed in by walls. High up in the hills, I felt like a bird flying through the sky.

We returned when darkness fell. Women lit fires and everybody gathered to hear what Moses had to say. This time, his older brother Aaron was with him too. Moses waited until everyone was quiet.

"God has heard your cries. He knows that you have suffered

too long under Pharaoh's rule, that your families have been taken from you into slavery, to toil and sweat in a land that is not your own. He knows that you are not free to worship Him. He will free you from bondage, and you will remember forever that it was He who brought you out of slavery. He will take you to the land he promised to our forefathers. The Lord has ordered me to go to Pharaoh and tell him that he is to let you go." His voice faltered and Aaron took over.

"My brother has poor speech—his tongue was burned when he was a child—but I am ready to speak on his behalf." That made everybody feel better. They knew Aaron. He wasn't a stranger like Moses.

One of the men rose. "Why should we believe anything this stranger says? We should cast him out! He is a danger to us. We're harboring a common criminal." The others murmured their agreement.

Another voice shouted, "Even if we could leave Egypt, where would we go? We can't just troop off into the wilderness. We'd be prey to thieves and wild animals—if we didn't starve or die of thirst first. It's madness! Are our lives not hard enough now? Why should we give up the little we have for an old, forgotten promise?"

Grandfather got to his feet, angrier than I had ever seen him before. "This is blasphemy! Has your spirit been crushed by these years of hard work and cruel treatment? The time has come for us to have a land of our own. This was God's promise to our forefathers!"

Nobody replied. They were already going back to their tents.

Moses and Aaron thanked Grandfather and turned to go, leaving him standing alone with me, looking up at the starry sky. I took his hand. "It really doesn't matter what they think, Grandfather. Pharaoh will never, ever release the people who are building his dream city," I said.

"That does not mean we should accept our bondage, child! Moses has been given a sacred mission. He and Aaron must try to convince our people. I may not live to see them succeed, but you must promise me, Dina, that when God's will is done and Pharaoh lets the Hebrews go, you will go with them."

I was shaking now. I did not want to disappoint my grandfather, but I had to tell the truth. "I can't promise that, Grandfather. I'm suited for the House of Weavers. How could I leave the court for the wilderness? How would I survive? I'm not strong enough to do as you ask."

"You will do what is right," he said.

The next morning Moses and Aaron were gone, and Grandfather did not speak of the Pharaoh again.

By the end of the week, I was ready to go back to the House of Weavers. I wanted to be back at my loom. Besides, I didn't feel that I belonged in Goshen. Had I simply been gone too long? Yes, I was a Hebrew and these were my people. I loved them. Their God was my God, so much more familiar to me than the many gods of the Egyptians, so many it was hard to keep track. But I didn't feel as if I belonged anymore. Many of the people I remembered from childhood were gone—taken into slavery, or dead. What was I to do? Even the coarse woolen clothing, the smells of dung and smoke, the bearded men had all become foreign to me. I could no longer feel at home in these dark tents. My mind was made up.

On my last night in Goshen, I lay awake in Grandfather's tent, thinking about how hard it was going to be to say goodbye to him. He was old now, and could not live much longer. It was hard to imagine I would ever see him again, and harder to accept that I would not. I couldn't think of words that would tell

him how much I loved him and how much I would miss him—
so I did a cowardly thing. As quietly as I could, I got dressed
and kissed his face. He did not wake when I slipped out of the
tent. In the dark, with nothing but the hooting of night birds for
company, I made my way back to Pi-Ramesses.

I got to the walls of the half-built city at dawn. I knew I
should hurry, but there was something I had to do first. Sheep
dung caked the hem of my cloak and my hair was in knots.
I wanted to wash before anybody saw me. We were going to
Faiyûm the next day. I wanted to be clean when I started my
new life.

I followed a path to the Nile and washed my long hair. I
was sitting on the bank, running my fingers through it to unknot
the tangles, when I heard a sound.

The Pharaoh, flanked by dozens of guards and accompanied
by his priests, had come to the river to perform the ritual in
worship of the crocodile-god, Sobek. I ducked down till the
water covered my shoulders, hoping that the reeds would hide
me. I tried to keep myself from swatting the mosquitoes that
buzzed around my head, and tried even harder not to believe
that the Pharaoh could somehow summon up a crocodile.

Suddenly I heard a rustling. The Pharaoh's guards heard it
too. They raised their spears. Two old, bearded men stepped
forward. They must have been standing on the bank all along,
hidden among the reeds. The Pharaoh raised his hand to stop
the guards from running their spears through the strangers. He
stared for a long moment.

"Moses? It can't be! What do you want here? My father was
merciful to you once, letting you escape. I may not feel disposed
to be so kind." His voice was not as harsh as his words.

Neither Moses nor Aaron bowed down as they should have, and the Pharaoh did not seem to expect it.

Moses spoke slowly so that his words would be clear. "Ramses, I have come to tell you to let my people go."

"Go?" The Pharaoh laughed.

"God has commanded me to tell you to release the Hebrews. We want to be free to worship God."

The guards hooted. Now Aaron spoke up angrily. "I will strike the waters of the Nile with my rod, and the river will turn to blood. All the fish will die. The Nile will reek so that you and your people will have nothing to drink."

I didn't wait to hear more. I had seen enough of the Pharaoh's magicians' tricks to know that such things could be conjured up, and I didn't want to find myself neck-deep in bloody water. I scrambled up the bank, my wet tunic slapping against my legs. The guards were so intent on Pharaoh that they didn't even see me scurry away.

Ora had been right. With all the excitement of the Festival, the only person who knew I had slipped away was the gatekeeper. And since he had been discovered at the end of the day by another guard drunk and asleep at his post, he was certainly not going to alert anyone to the fact that a slave had escaped on his watch. I think he was relieved, and not just a little surprised, to see that I had returned at last.

It was back to work for the weavers now, and all day at my loom I puzzled over what I had seen on the banks of the Nile. Neither Moses nor Aaron had bowed down to Pharaoh. They had stood up to him, face to face, stood up to this man whom the Egyptians considered a god. That was not just bold—it was rebellious. I couldn't believe that anyone could be so brave. Somehow I knew that the matter was not finished, and I wondered what Moses would do next. But I had to accept that I probably would never know, because the next day I would be leaving the court with the Queen and the other favored slaves, headed to Faiyûm.

I had packed up my loom for the journey south and was saying my goodbyes to the other slaves when one of the Queen's attendants appeared. "Something strange has happened," she told the doorkeeper. "All the fish are dying. You can't believe what it smells like. The Queen's delaying her move for a week because it's not possible to travel through this horrible stench!"

All I could do was set up my loom again.

There was much talk of dying fish but none of letting the Hebrews go free. I wasn't surprised. Who would have believed that Moses would come back to a place where he was a wanted man, much less that he would dare to make demands of the Pharaoh? Nevertheless, a few days later I heard one of the Queen's attendants speaking to the doorkeeper.

"That traitor, Moses, has turned up in court. He says the Pharaoh must release the Hebrews from bondage or the whole world will be covered with frogs, of all things! Can you believe it?"

"Preposterous!" The doorkeeper glared at me when he realized I was listening. I couldn't believe it either, but I shivered nonetheless.

Moses' threat was not an idle one. Suddenly frogs were everywhere: in the bedchambers and in the beds, even in the ovens and baking bowls. It was disgusting. Almost as soon as it happened—news spread fast in Pharaoh's court—we heard that Pharaoh had summoned Moses and promised this time to let the Hebrews go if only the plague of frogs would stop. Sure enough, by the next day, heaps of *dead* frogs were everywhere. The dead frogs were even more disgusting than the live ones.

A load of newly spun thread was delivered to the House of
Weavers. As we stacked it, I consoled myself with the thought,
I will be far away by the time this is woven. But once again the
Queen's attendant sent word that the move to Faiyûm had been
postponed. The Queen was refusing to go out of doors because
of the dead frogs.

After that the troubles came faster and faster, like the blows
of a hammer. Maybe because of the dead fish and rotting frogs,
clouds of biting insects filled the air. Soon the livestock started
to die. The decomposing carcasses and the insects made people
ill. They got boils all over their bodies. Maybe the Pharaoh's
magicians could have found a magic to heal the boils, but they
didn't because they were covered in boils themselves.

Then hail fell, as big as stones, flattening what wheat and
flax had not already been chewed up by the insects.

Word reached the palace that, for some reason, Goshen had
been spared the plagues. This infuriated the Egyptians, who now
blamed the Hebrews for all their suffering. On the day we were
ordered to weave more cloth in which to wrap the dead, the doorkeeper shoved me hard as I got up to get thread for my loom.

"You Hebrews have brought these plagues down on us! The
gods must be angry because you did not worship them properly
at the Festival. How dare this Moses ask the Pharaoh, in the
name of his God, to set the Hebrews free? How dare he even
speak to the Pharaoh? Pharaoh is a god himself! He will do as
he pleases. And it pleases him that the Hebrews are slaves."

I was terrified. It was as if there was a deadly, horrible battle
being fought between a man who thought he was a god and the
God of everything.

Next came locusts, so many of them that not a scrap of land
could be seen. Locusts carpeted everything. They ate every
blade of grass, every piece of fruit from the trees. Then we
heard that Moses had once again pleaded with Pharaoh, and

once again Pharaoh had agreed to release the slaves. As soon as he did, a west wind blew all the locusts away.

By evening the locusts were gone. The Queen's attendants gathered those of us she'd chosen—makeup artists, hairdressers, seamstresses, spinners—and told us, "We go to Faiyûm at daybreak. Be ready!" Carts pulled by oxen were lined up in the palace grounds. We scrambled to pack them with our tools and waited for daylight.

But once again, Pharaoh had changed his mind. Then a plague of darkness was upon us. The dawn didn't come. The hours passed, and still the sun didn't rise. It was darker than night because no stars shone. I couldn't tell if my eyes were open or shut. It was unnatural, terrifying. Nobody dared to move far. All we could do was grope our way to the clay jugs that held drinking water.

I'm not sure how many hours passed before the Queen herself arrived, surrounded by lanterns.

"I have had enough of delays," she said, a note of panic in her voice. "We are leaving by lantern light!" The lanterns helped, but the darkness was still so thick that we could barely see the line of carts that creaked under all the Queen's belongings. We would be on our way at last, but I was too dazed, too frightened, to be excited.

Finally, someone thought to hang oil lamps from the statues of gods that lined the palace grounds, so that we were encircled by a dim glow. The gods' empty eyes stared. They had not protected the people from suffering.

The carts were about to roll when the darkness was pierced by a terrible cry. I have never heard anything worse. Someone screamed, "The children are dying! The Pharaoh's own son is dead!"

I covered my ears. Weeping people poured out of the buildings and into the broad palace grounds. The lanterns couldn't light the whole vast space. I was afraid to move in the panic.

A strong hand grabbed my shoulder. One of the lanterns flickered and in the faint light I could see that it was Ora.

Then, over the chaos, I heard Moses' voice. The crowd parted as he and his brother Aaron walked with steady steps away from Pharaoh's palace.

"Hebrews!" he called, his voice growing more clear with every word. "We are free to leave Egypt. Pharaoh has released us at last. We must go now! Follow me!"

I froze. I did not want to follow an old man into the unknown, into the unnatural night, into the deadly wilderness. I wanted to go to Faiyûm with the Queen, where I would be comfortable, where I would be safe.

Ora shook me. "Listen, Dina. You are free!"

"I am on my way to Faiyûm," I protested.

"Don't you understand? Moses is leading your people out of Egypt. Don't you know what that means? Do you want to live the rest of your life as nothing but the Queen's cat? If it were me, I would give anything to be back among my own people, back where people love me."

I understood what she meant. I knew that I would never be anything more than a slave here, grateful for any scrap of praise, living among strangers, observing *their* customs and worshipping *their* gods, to be used and eventually forgotten. I meant nothing to these people.

I thought of my grandfather's words: *You will do what is right.* But I was so afraid. Then I remembered the scene at the river. Moses must have wished that he too could go back to his peaceful life as a shepherd, but instead he stood up to Pharaoh. He refused to bow down. He delivered God's message.

I embraced Ora. "Thank you, my dear friend." This time I was the one who whispered, "Courage!"

I pushed through the crowd and joined the line of Hebrews who'd been slaves in the stables and workshops. Was my father out there with the builders? Would he risk leaving Pi-Ramesses? I shivered, though the air was as steamy as ever. When we reached the towering gates, I felt nothing but fear.

I thought of trying to find a way back to the Queen's caravan. I didn't know how to be free. Then I thought about Moses striding ahead of us. Though he did not want to carry out what God had asked of him, he did not turn away. And now I knew the answer to Ora's parting question.

"No, Ora. I would rather be a lion and free!"

EPILOGUE

The Hebrews wandered for years before they reached the land where they could settle, establish their rulers, and worship God. Though their time in the wilderness was full of hardship and doubt, it was also during that time that they received the Ten Commandments, which became the basis for a way of life that has lasted for thousands of years.

Moses died before he could enter the Promised Land.

MATTAN

The sheep bleated and jostled one another as my sister, Nirit, drew water from the well. "Hurry up and drink, my lambs," she said to them as she poured the water into the trough. "It'll soon be dark." I don't know whether or not they understood, but Nirit liked to talk to the flock anyway.

To me she added, "Mother will be furious if we're late."

Tough little Nirit wasn't afraid of anything except our mother's angry tongue—and Mother would be very angry if we didn't get home by sundown. Sundown marked the start of Sabbath, when no work was to be done. Nirit was right—we had to hurry if we were to get home in time. Besides, we were hungry. During the week we had so little to eat that our simple Sabbath dinner tasted like a feast.

I whistled to our old sheepdog, Shua. As he yipped at the flock to move them to the night pen, I shielded my eyes against the late afternoon sun, looking to see if any lambs had strayed. I saw five men wearing linen tunics marching toward us.

"Nirit, I think they're Roman soldiers!" I grabbed her arm and pulled her off to the side of the road, where we'd be out of their way. I didn't want to give them any excuse to find fault with us. Though it was getting late, and I was frightened, I was also curious. Curious the way I was when I found a scorpion in the sand.

We stood at the roadside, watching. "Please, let's go, Mattan," said my sister. "The sheep are starting to stray."

I ignored her. I was fascinated by the Romans because they were so different from anything I knew. We didn't even speak the same language: they spoke Latin and we spoke Aramaic. And the Romans weren't Jews like us. They didn't worship the one God. They prayed to many gods.

More than that, they were powerful, and we had learned to fear them. The Romans had come with their army and taken over our land. They'd even chosen our king for us. And they forced us to pay taxes so high that we were left with almost nothing. And they were brutal to anyone who even spoke out against them. It was said that even looking at a Roman soldier the wrong way might be enough to earn you a smack across the face or a hobnailed boot to your backside.

Years before, their general, Pompey, had ordered his troops to lay siege to our capital city, Jerusalem. The poor citizens of the city fled to the Temple, seeking safety within its strong walls. For three long months they held out against Rome, until there was no more food and water and they starved. Twelve thousand people died in that siege. And the Romans finished off the rest with their cruel swords: the blood of men and women and children ran in the streets.

As the soldiers approached, we saw puffs of dust rising around their gleaming leather sandals, and we could hear them singing a boisterous song. Scary as they were, it was hard not to be impressed by the gleaming daggers tucked into their leather belts.

Just then, one of our sheep bolted into the road, right in front of the soldiers. Shua chased after it and tried frantically to bring it back to the flock, but a soldier, impatient with the moment's delay, kicked the old dog in the ribs. Shua sailed through the air and landed, whimpering, on the stony edge of the road.

Nirit jerked her arm from my grasp and shouted out, "You stop it!" She scrambled over the stony ground, falling and gashing her knee. The soldiers just roared with laughter.

I was furious that the Roman had kicked our gentle Shua, and I was mortified, too, that Nirit was crying like a baby right in front of them. *If I had a dagger of my own, I would show them!* I thought. But instead I just stood there, helpless, until the Romans passed.

Gingerly, Shua got to her feet and shook herself.

"See, Nirit, Shua's all right," I reassured her. But Nirit didn't answer. Her knee was bleeding badly.

Somehow we managed to get the flock to their night pen. When we were finished, I picked up Nirit and carried her tenderly, as if she were one of my own lambs, and together we stumbled toward home, her blood wetting my shoulder.

We got home just as the sun was going down. Mother had already lit the Sabbath candles. She'd swept up the flakes of dung and mud that always fell from the walls of our home, and she'd watered the sweet herbs that made the house smell fresh for the Sabbath.

She was waiting in the doorway for us, and I could see from her expression that she was ready to scold us, but when she saw that Nirit was hurt, her anger vanished. Tenderly, she took my sister from me.

"Fetch water from the courtyard so I can wash her wound," she said.

Later, as I scrubbed my face and washed my feet in a basin, I could hear my mother speaking softly to Nirit. I felt terrible. If I hadn't been so curious about the Roman soldiers, Nirit would not have been hurt.

The Sabbath was supposed to be a day of rest, but my thoughts were in a muddle. I was angry at the Romans for their cruelty. But mostly, I was ashamed. I hadn't taken care of Nirit. I was afraid that my older brothers and my parents would blame me for putting us both in danger, and for the ugly gash on Nirit's knee. Sometimes a cut like that, if it didn't heal quickly, could get much worse instead of better—it could make you very sick. I prayed that wouldn't be the case for my sister.

For the next few days, I went to the pasture with the sheep alone. Nirit's knee was red and swollen and she couldn't walk very far. But every morning she asked our father again if she could come with me. And he always told her that if she got up early, she could walk with our mother to the village oven to bake our bread, but no farther.

On the third day after our run-in with the Romans, I woke to find my brothers had already risen and gone to farm our fields. I washed, and laced my sandals, and said my morning prayers, thinking that a day in the peaceful company of the sheep might soothe my troubled mind.

Father was squatting in the courtyard, muttering to himself and making calculations in the dirt with a stick. "If our farm produces a hundred sacks of grain, we'll have to set aside twenty to feed the animals. We have to save ten sacks for seed at the next harvest. And now we have to give fifty sacks to the Romans as taxes! That leaves almost nothing to feed us. What a choice! Pay the taxes and starve now, or sell the land, pay our taxes, and starve later."

He noticed me standing in the doorway. "Don't mind me, Mattan." He sounded defeated. "I always believed that if I worked hard, your lives would be better than my own. But if things go on this way, I will have nothing to give you. Nothing at all."

"Maybe the Messiah will come and save us, Father." It was Nirit. I hadn't noticed her lying on a mat in the shade of an awning. I felt a knot of fear grow in my chest. Pus was seeping through the cloth Mother had bound around Nirit's knee. An angry red line marked her leg. I stooped to kiss her forehead. It was burning. "Maybe the Messiah will make the Romans leave us be," she said.

"That's right, Father. Maybe the Messiah will be a warrior like King David, and he'll lead us in a charge that will conquer the Romans." I brandished my shepherd's crook like a sword, trying to make Nirit laugh.

Father smiled. "From your lips to God's ears. As for me, I dream about a Messiah, an anointed one, as the prophet Isaiah promised, who not only will deliver us from our enemies but will bring justice to the world." He stopped to offer Nirit a sip of water and to brush her damp hair from her forehead. "Enough of this. Mattan, the sheep are waiting. Nirit, today you will rest at home. I don't want you sneaking off to follow your brother." His voice caught in his throat. Until then I hadn't noticed how worried he was.

"I want to stay with Nirit."

"No, the sheep need you. Mother has gone to fetch the healer. You can help us all by tending to the flock."

Reluctantly, I whistled to Shua and set off to take the sheep to pasture.

Alone all day with no one to talk to except Shua and the sheep, I missed Nirit. I thought about the funny little songs she invented to make me laugh. She had given all the sheep names, and she liked to make up stories about them. All that day I made up stories of my own, so I would have something to give her when I got home, something to make her smile. At least I could look forward to that.

When I returned at nightfall, I knew something was terribly wrong. I didn't see my father or my brothers, and my mother wasn't there to greet me. Instead, a neighbor met me in the doorway of our home.

She wiped her eyes. "May God comfort you among the mourners of Zion." It was the ancient greeting for those who have lost a loved one.

I howled and pushed past her. My brothers and my father sat on the dirt floor, red-eyed.

"Nirit? Is it Nirit?" I cried.

I fell into my mother's arms. "My poor baby," she whispered. For a moment, I thought she meant me. "One less mouth to feed," she said. "May God forgive me." Then her tears came.

"Out of the question! I forbid it." Father rose angrily to his feet, but I wasn't afraid. I was just fourteen, but already I was taller than him. "Your duty lies here!"

I would not listen. Week had followed dreary week. It seemed that spring would never come, and all I could think of was escaping. As Mother had said, these were times when one less mouth to feed was a blessing. Besides, there wasn't much land left to till, and any small boy could tend the few sheep we had left. This was what I told myself. The truth was that I had bigger plans for myself. No wonder the Roman soldiers treated us with such scorn: we put up with being taxed into poverty and selling our land just to stay alive. That wasn't going to be me anymore. I was going to go out into the world and take whatever I wanted, just like them. And I couldn't bear being in a house that had grown bleak without Nirit's laughter.

"So you're leaving us, and for what? To make your fortune and come back like a hero? You'll find out—there is as much grief and as little glory waiting for you out there as you ever found here. It would be braver for you to stay here and help your family."

Mother was more frightened than angry. "Mattan, people are desperate. There are bandits everywhere. What if you fall in with bad company, with rebels?"

"I won't, Mother. I promise."

Mother and Father were always warning us to stay away from rebels. I knew they didn't mean our friends and neighbors, though I suppose you could have called them rebels too. We all knew plenty of people in Galilee who rebelled in small, secret ways against those who collected taxes for the Romans—a thumb on the scales when they were weighing their spices, working slowly when they were forced to build the roads, pretending that they didn't understand orders barked at them in Latin.

No, the rebels my parents feared were those who talked about open, armed uprisings against the Romans. I had heard too many stories about how the Romans dealt with those who rebelled openly against their harsh laws. They killed those who tried to rise against them, or they made them slaves.

"I don't want to fight against the Romans," I said. "But I don't want to be under anyone's heel, either. And if I stay here, I'll have no choice. There's nothing more to say. I'm leaving."

My father stroked Shua's head. "I can't fight you anymore. I'm too tired. Do what you have to do." He laid his hands on my head and blessed me. Then he held me in his arms. "Promise me you'll stay safe, my boy. Hard times make for dangerous times."

It was still early morning, and the rising sun was turning the mud-and-stone houses of Nazareth a warm pink. I looked down the stony little street, where just about everybody I had ever known lived. I would miss them, but I wanted more from life than they had, and I was determined to find it.

I set out down the road, pretending that my staff was a Roman lance. I knew where I was headed: the large town a half day's walk away. There was building going on and over the years many of the men in our village found work. Truth be told, I'd had this plan in the back of my head since I was just a small boy, when our neighbor Joseph and his son Jesus had gone there to work. But then, Jesus and Joseph were both carpenters, good ones. I started to get nervous. I hoped they'd still need workers on the building sites. Would they need one whose only skill was herding sheep?

The town was like another world to me. I stood at the end of the broad main street, confused and delighted by the bustle. I tried to take it all in: the rowdy cries of the shopkeepers as they set out their wares for the day, the sharp, sweet smells of spices, the reds and blues and rich yellows of bolts of cloth, the mounds of dried fruits that made my mouth water. I wandered up and down the streets, gaping at the public baths and the theater and the tall houses until my empty stomach reminded me why I was there.

I noticed a half-finished building covered in scaffolding. Men scurried up and down it like ants. "What are they building here?" I asked a man who was mixing mortar in a bucket.

He answered without looking up. "A synagogue, and a fancy one at that. The patron is one of those who have grown rich by serving the Romans."

"Is there work here?" Hunger made me brave.

He laid down the stick he'd been using and looked at me for the first time. "What can you do?"

I felt my pack digging into my shoulders. "Carry," I said.

That was how I found myself carrying bricks and tools up a ramp and then down again. When night came, I followed a group of workers to their rough camp. They shared their pot of lentils with me. I wrapped my cloak around myself and was asleep before I had a chance to think about home.

I worked hard. At first I was too exhausted to listen to the chatter of the older men; it was all I could do to keep from tripping on the wobbly ramp and dropping an armload of bricks. One day, our patron, the man who was paying for the synagogue, came to the site. I stared at him. He looked odd. At first I didn't know why. Then I realized that where his cheekbones should have been, there was flesh filling out his smooth, shiny skin. I couldn't remember ever seeing somebody who wasn't as thin as a blade of grass.

He gave an order: we were to hang a silver eagle from the roof.

The foreman stepped forward. "Perhaps, sir, another type of ornament . . .?"

One sharp look from the patron silenced him.

The eagle was the symbol of Rome. It was on their buildings, their weapons, and even their coins. The patron wanted it displayed to show the Romans that he was loyal to them. What he was showing us was that he was nothing but a lapdog of the Romans, ready to do anything they wished. No wonder—by wringing taxes from the poor for them, he was growing very rich.

That night in the camp, the workers talked of nothing else. "This is awful! It's bad enough that the Romans' taxes take bread out of our children's mouths. Now we are supposed to be reminded of their power even when we go into the synagogue to pray to God! It is an outrage!"

One of the workers gathered up a handful of twigs to make a fire. He placed ten of them on the ground. "Here we are, the Jews of Galilee. We're the bottom of the heap." He placed five bigger sticks on top of the first ones. "These are the local rulers, like that fat frog of a man who's building the synagogue." We laughed as he chose an even heavier stick and laid it on top of the pile. "Then there is our Jewish king, Herod, on top of that. Our king? That's rich! He was appointed by the Romans because they know that if they say 'Jump' he'll say 'How high?'"

He had saved the biggest stick for last. He jammed it onto the pile of kindling. "And here's Rome, crushing everything beneath!" He set the pile on fire.

The workmen hatched a plan. A disastrous one.

We waited for the new moon, when the sky was at its darkest, and then we crept to the half-built synagogue. The two tallest men hoisted themselves on the scaffolding and tore down the silver eagle. We stifled a cheer as they hurled it to the ground. We each took a turn stomping on it until it was nothing but a misshapen lump of metal.

The next day at the building site, everyone acted as if nothing had happened. I told myself that nobody had noticed the eagle was missing. As the day grew hotter, I realized that I had forgotten my water skin. I ran back to the camp to fetch it.

I was returning when the Roman soldiers rushed by me. They descended on the workers, their swords flashing. Terrified, I flattened myself against the wall of the house next door to the synagogue. Someone had dragged a huge clay plot outside.

Quickly, I wedged myself into it. Something wet covered my feet. I realized I was crouching up to my knees in wine.

Inside the synagogue I could hear the men screaming for mercy, but mercy had no meaning to those Roman soldiers. The workmen's pleas became shrieks and groans. Then there was nothing but silence—and that was almost worse.

I waited until I couldn't bear the cramping in my legs. Sodden with wine, praying that the Romans were gone, I hoisted myself up.

Cautiously, I picked my way through what was left of the synagogue. The walls were splattered with blood. Death was no stranger in Nazareth. I had seen my share of dead babies and terribly mangled farmers. I'd sat by Nirit's still body, reciting psalms through my tears, until her grave was dug. But I'd seen nothing like this. There had been fifty men alive this morning. Now there were none.

I tried not to look at the bodies, contorted in anguish. The stench was unbearable. Dogs were already scavenging among the corpses. One man, the one who'd hired me, lay on his side as if he were asleep under a blanket. The blanket moved. When I realized it was a sheet of iridescent flies, I vomited.

I thought people would come running. Nobody did. The workmen were beyond help. There was no point in riling the Romans further.

Tormented by the flies that swarmed around my sticky hair and clothes, I chose a road that led to the Galilee and I ran, heedless of the sights and sounds around me. I could think of only one thing: getting away. At the water's edge, I rinsed myself off as best I could and lay down trembling on the stony beach. Not to think, but to try to forget.

"Boy! You there! Would you like to earn a bowl of soup?"

I squinted against the sun, too numb to be frightened. Before me stood a tiny man, as neat as a cat, but as old and tough as a silvery olive tree. He'd tied a donkey to a bush that grew near the bank. The donkey was thoughtfully chewing on leaves.

The old man peered at me. "Is something wrong? Are you lame?"

"No."

"Good! Can you *act* lame?"

"I suppose so. Why?"

"Ever hear of Jacob the Magnificent?"

I shook my head.

Although the little man looked disappointed, you couldn't say he was surprised. "I need a boy for my show. You look pitiful enough. My last boy left me for parts unknown. If you'll let me heal you every night, you can come along with me and my good old girl Devash." The donkey turned her head when she heard her name.

I didn't get a chance to answer. Even if I'd wanted to, I wouldn't have been able to say anything because Jacob the Magnificent didn't stop talking.

"Some call me a cheat or a swindler, but I like to think of myself as a simple trader. I learned all kinds of sales tricks from my father, and if you've a quick mind I can teach them to you too: how to slip a thumb on scales, how to top up jars of perfume with water, how to mix tonics and medicines, how to tell a story so well that folks think they have to have whatever it is I'm selling."

His words had a strange effect on me. Each thing he said seemed to dull one of the day's dreadful memories. Luckily for me, Jacob was happy to keep talking.

"For years I've wandered the length and breadth of Judea and Galilee. I've climbed the mist-topped mountains in the north and crossed the mean, stony deserts in the south. I've seen the soft green valleys and cooled my face with the sea winds on the sea coast. Oh, the sights I've seen! Shall I tell you about the sacred crocodiles that swim in the Nile?" I nodded and I listened, drugged by the sound of his voice. "I will tell you about the giraffes and fierce white rhinoceroses in the zoo at Alexandria. If only you could see Queen Cleopatra's barge. Why, it has an aquarium, and a gymnasium, and a garden, and even stables. All on a boat, mind!"

I couldn't bear to go back to the town. It wasn't just the horror of what had happened there—I was worried that somebody might tell the Romans that they'd overlooked me when they slaughtered the other workmen. Besides, there was something about the odd little man that I liked. When Jacob finally paused for breath, I said, "Yes."

"Yes what?" He'd already forgotten his invitation.

"Yes, I'll be your lame boy," I said.

"Splendid."

Jacob helped me to my feet and I plodded along beside Devash until we reached a village not much bigger than Nazareth. Jacob found a shady spot for Devash and untied the baskets of trinkets and cheap pots that hung in clattering bundles on her back. He spread his tattered carpet on the ground.

"Go hide and don't come out until I say, 'Does anybody else need my help?' That's your cue. Understand?"

I crouched behind Devash while Jacob banged a pot and cried, "Come one, come all! Miracles and bargains galore. Miracles and bargains!"

The villagers, still dusty from a day working under the hot Galilean sun, gathered in the village square. They sat on the ground and waited expectantly for the show to begin.

"Ask me for a miracle, ladies and gentlemen. Jacob the Magnificent will oblige."

"Is there a tonic that will bring back my husband's fine head of hair?" a woman called out. The other women hooted.

"Of course, my dear lady." Jacob bowed. "An elixir made of equal parts burnt mouse, burnt tooth of a nag, and a burnt rag, mixed nice and smooth with bear's grease and powdered deer bone, will do the trick. Rub it on your husband's head until the hair grows back, lush as a boy's. You may be in luck! I think I happen to have a vial of it with me." He fished around in one of the baskets. "Aha!" He held up a blue glass jar. The villagers howled their approval. "Is there anyone else who needs my help?"

That was my cue. I rubbed Devash's velvety nose for luck and hobbled into the square, leaning on the wooden crutch Jacob had provided.

"I am a poor lame boy wishing to be cured." My voice boomed, making everybody jump. Jacob's eyebrows drew together.

"I hope I can help this poor child." Jacob rolled his eyes heavenward. Then he held out a leather flask to me, muttering, "You're supposed to be feeble. Act feeble!"

The liquid tasted of wine and honey. I was about to take another swig, but he pulled the flask away. The villagers watched in silence. Jacob said through gritted teeth, "I wonder if he is deserving of the secret properties of this miraculous potion?"

I finally remembered what Jacob had told me to do. With a whoop, I straightened up and tossed away my crutch. "I can walk!" I cried. "It's a miracle!"

The villagers cheered. I thought the show would end then, but nobody made a move to leave. They wanted more.

Jacob asked them, "Would you like to hear a story?" They shouted that they would. "What will be your pleasure, then? An old tale or a new?"

"Pompey in Egypt, please," they cried. The fate of Pompey

was a popular tale. Everyone remembered the siege of Jerusalem and the misery he'd brought to them. We all loved to hear about his gruesome death.

Jacob sat cross-legged on his carpet and let his voice weave its magic. "Friends, we all know that the Romans are a brutal lot. Ten years after that hot day when Pompey entered Jerusalem, there was a bitter rivalry between two great generals to see who would be the supreme ruler of Rome. Would it be Julius Caesar or Pompey the Great? It was Caesar who won and became emperor. Pompey was left with nothing. Where could he hide?"

"Egypt!" said the villagers.

Jacob nodded. The air cooled as he told a complicated tale of intrigue and betrayal. The villagers hung on every word until the sky had grown dark. Jacob hurried to finish his story. "Egypt didn't work out well for Pompey." This made the crowd guffaw. "He was stabbed to death right in front of his whole army"—the audience cheered as Jacob ran his finger across his throat—"and his head was chopped off!"

After the show was over, Jacob shared a slightly squashed spinach pie with me. "Well, I call that a successful evening's work, don't you?" He rubbed Devash's ear, wished her good night, and we all settled down to sleep.

That's how I became a professional lame boy, and sometimes, for a change, a blind one. Through the hot months of that summer, I travelled with Jacob all over the Galilee. Though we sometimes went without dinner, it was thrilling to see some of the things I'd always dreamed of. I saw the broad roads the Romans built, their clever aqueducts for carrying water, and the towns that the Romans and their rich friends were transforming with their lavish houses and marble baths and theaters. It was amazing, impressive, and sometimes I had to remind myself that I hated the Romans for what they were doing to us, because all these marvels came at a terrible cost: taxes that were causing so much misery, the dying cries of the rebellious workmen I had heard. I asked Jacob if a person could admire something and hate it at the same time. He didn't have an answer for me.

Devash looked at us reproachfully as we coaxed her to hurry along the rutted road that ran along the shore to a fishing village Jacob knew. He was even more talkative than usual.

"Wait until we get to Capernaum! It's on the shores of a lake, so we'll be able to wash off the day's dirt."

Actually, it was the dirt of more days than I could count, but I didn't say so. I scratched at my flea bites.

"If we get there before dark, we can have a nice swim," he promised. "Yes, a swim first, and then a fat roasted fish in exchange for our show. Perfection! Move along, Devash, old girl."

Capernaum was only a dusty collection of mud-and-stone houses, but it was luxurious compared with some of the inland villages we'd seen. For one thing, the usual stench of pee—and more—was missing, thanks to a system they had to wash waste away.

Once we'd had our swim and had fed and watered Devash, we headed toward the village, ready to give a show. A small group had already gathered at the foot of a hill.

"Ah, our fame has spread!" I was pleased.

Jacob snorted. "I don't think so—they can't have known we were coming. So who are they here to see? It looks like some other showman got here first. He'll have first crack at their money. Rotten luck!"

"Maybe we should keep going while it's still light," I said, but Jacob was already elbowing his way to the front.

"Lesson of the day: no harm in seeing the competition, boy. Watch closely."

A man sat on the hill, speaking to the rapt villagers. Two men shifted on the ground to make room for us.

"Who's this fellow?" Jacob asked one of them.

Without taking his eyes off the speaker, the man answered, "He's Jesus."

Jesus of Nazareth! I had been only a small boy when Jesus left Nazareth, so I wouldn't have recognized him. I'd heard Mother talk about what an unusually wise child he'd been and what a fine carpenter he had become. Now here he was, sitting on the ground the way rabbis did when they were teaching. Seeing him gave me a pang of homesickness.

I waited for some tricks, some bragging about superior merchandise, but there was none. Instead, he taught. In a sure, strong voice, Jesus talked about mercy and love, and how these were mightier than force and violence. He talked about the Kingdom of God and how everything in the world was part of it, even the Romans. Then he said a prayer that started, "Our Father, who art in Heaven . . ."

I listened, but his words confused me. Jesus was saying that it was humble people who would one day inherit the earth. Could this be right? Could any "humble" man ever take on the Romans and win? He talked about a life after this one, a life in Heaven. Did that mean that I would see Nirit again someday? The pain that I always felt when I thought about her eased a bit. Quickly, I wiped my tears away.

Night fell and the villagers drifted away to their homes, but a group of men and women, old and young, clustered around Jesus. I was surprised that Jacob was lingering with them.

I hung back. "Let's go," I said. "I'm hungry." I tugged on Jacob's arm. Truth be told, I suddenly felt shy. I didn't want Jesus to see me. If by some chance he recognized me, or heard that I was also from Nazareth, Jesus might know who I was and wonder why I wasn't being a dutiful son, working on my father's land. I guess I was ashamed.

One of Jesus' followers must have heard us, because he asked if we would like to share their food and stay with them for the night. I was astonished when Jacob said yes.

"Might as well find out what this fellow's attraction is," he said to me as we led Devash to their camp.

We found the man who had invited us to stay—his name, he told us, was Peter—tending a cooking fire. Jacob squatted beside him. "Ever heard of Jacob the Magnificent?"

"Ah, yes." Peter didn't look up.

"I heal people, you know!"

Peter just smiled and went on tending the fire.

Jacob tried again. "Tell us about Jesus."

Now Peter was eager to talk. "Jesus has been going from village to village throughout the Galilee for some time. Capernaum is my home, and when Jesus first came here, my brother Andrew and I were so impressed that we left our fishing nets in order to learn from him. Now we go with him, listening to him teach and watching him heal."

"Heal?" Jacob snorted.

Peter gave him a level look. "My mother-in-law was burning up with fever. We had given her up for dead. Jesus touched her hand and the fever left her. She was brought back to life. People say that he performed a miracle that day. I'm surprised you haven't heard of him."

I couldn't resist. "I have!" I piped up, and Jacob looked miffed that for once I knew something he didn't. "I'm from Nazareth too. Is Jesus still a carpenter?" I said it to show off.

"No, he's no longer a carpenter," replied Peter.

"Well, if he's that good, I suppose people pay him well for healing," said Jacob.

"He takes no money for his teaching or for his healing, but people are generous, especially the women you see around here. They have a bit of money of their own. They help out so that Jesus can focus on his work. The rest of us take on day jobs when we can, and everyone shares with one another. Jesus jokes that we are like one big family, eating and drinking together and squabbling amongst ourselves!"

I didn't mean to blurt out what I was thinking. "What a life!"

Peter laughed ruefully. "I fear that the time is coming when this will be a hard life, perhaps a dangerous one. Jesus is making enemies."

"Enemies?" I interrupted, but before I could say more, Peter went on to explain.

"He keeps getting into debates with learned men, rabbis, about how to follow Jewish laws." He poked at the fire with a stick. "Jesus seems to go out of his way to irritate them. Listen to this. Just the other day a small band of us were walking with Jesus through a grain field. We complained that we were hungry, so Jesus had us pick some heads of grain to munch on."

I was puzzled. "What's wrong with that? It's the custom. The Torah tells us that we are always supposed to leave some of our crop behind for those who need it. Farmers let travelers do it all the time. My father allows it, and we have hardly any to spare."

"It was the Sabbath! Picking grain is like harvesting, and the Torah says we can't work on the day of rest. The rabbis were furious. Jesus pointed out that the temple priests work on the Sabbath, so why should it matter that we picked grain? That made matters worse. Now there are those who call him names, saying that he's doing the devil's work. These days it is not prudent to make enemies of the powerful, and make no mistake—some of these rabbis have power. I fear that each of these angry debates is like a twig feeding a flame."

Jacob helped Peter hoist a pot of soup onto the fire. "At least he's not making enemies of the Romans."

"Not yet he isn't, but the day will come. Jesus' heart is with the poor, those who are only a few bowls of watery soup away from starvation. Do you think the Romans are going to be pleased when they hear that somebody is telling the sick, the weak, the poor that they have a right to be happy? The right to a share in God's Kingdom? When Jesus talks about a new kind of government where only God is in charge, where does that leave Rome? Jesus is telling people that they must be loyal to the Kingdom of Heaven and not to Rome. How long do you think the Romans will stand for that, especially if it means people might decide to stop paying their taxes? They would blame him for stirring up a rebellion."

I thought of the awful buzzing of flies clustered on murdered bodies and squeezed my eyes shut to blur the memory.

I heard Jacob's voice. "Speaking up against injustice can be as dangerous as armed rebellion, when power lies with the unjust."

"It's true. I thought Jesus would be more cautious after what happened to John the Baptist. John was a prophet. People came to him to be immersed in water—a ritual to wash away their sins. Jesus asked John to purify him in the Jordan River.

John was attracting a lot of followers, who were stirring up rebellious talk. King Herod had him arrested and ordered that his head be cut off. I thought Jesus would be frightened, but it hasn't stopped him from speaking out at all. He seems more determined than ever to preach what he says is the word of God."

The stars were coming out. Jacob looked for a place for us to spread our cloaks. Around us, the men sat in groups and talked quietly while the women turned the fish roasting on the campfires and passed bowls of stewed lentils, chunks of bread, and trays of dates. Jesus was nowhere to be seen. When I asked, somebody told me that after a long day Jesus often disappeared to rest and to pray alone.

We didn't see Jesus the next morning when we thanked Peter and hoisted our last remaining pots onto Devash's strong back. Jacob calculated the date on his fingers. "It's market day in the village up the road. Good thing. We could use more stock."

A wintry wind was blowing. We made good time because Devash's pack was lighter than usual. As we trudged along on either side of the donkey, Jacob was telling me a gory story about Cleopatra, the queen of Egypt, how she'd married one of her brothers and then waged war against him, and then she'd married another of her brothers and poisoned him. I was trying hard to keep it all straight, so I didn't notice the bandits until they were on us. There were three of them, ragged and desperate. They must have seen our light packs and reasoned that loaded baskets had been exchanged for a purse full of coins. One grabbed Devash's bridle and ordered us to halt. The other put Jacob into a headlock and snatched the small leather purse that hung around the old man's neck.

"Let them take everything except Devash!" Jacob's words were strangled.

Rage pounded so hard in my ears that I didn't—I couldn't—listen. I had grown to love that tiny old man, and nobody was going to hurt him!

I launched myself at the third bandit. The two of us fell to the ground, clawing at each other. I clutched a handful of scraggly beard. I heard a crack and felt hot blood, so I knew my nose was broken, but I didn't care about the pain. I could see that the man who'd been holding Devash was trying to lead her away. She bucked, her eyes rolling in terror. I butted my opponent as hard as I could with my head. His head banged against the packed earth. His grip loosened for a moment and I lurched to my feet.

"You let her go!" I screamed at the bandit. I snatched up a stone and threw it. With a yelp, he fell to his knees.

They'd had enough of me, and besides, they already had Jacob's purse. As quickly as they'd appeared, the bandits were gone.

Devash was shivering with fright. Jacob soothed her with whispers and gentle pats. Gingerly, I felt my swollen nose.

Once Jacob had calmed Devash, he turned to me, all business. He reached into one of the baskets that still hung from Devash's back and pulled out a potion. He dabbed the nasty-smelling stuff on my nose and stanched the blood.

"I think we've earned ourselves a rest, don't you?" said Jacob. We found a spot out in an open field, in sight of a farmer and his son who were harvesting winter wheat. Nobody would be able to take us by surprise there. I watched with a heavy heart as the farmer stopped and ruffled his boy's hair.

We passed the wineskin between us. Jacob said, "So you are a fighter, Mattan."

"I suppose I know how to use my fists," I boasted. "And did you see me butt him with my head? Bam!"

"There are better ways to use your head."

I was annoyed. I had expected praise, not a lecture. My nose was throbbing. I had a bump the size of a fist growing on my forehead. I was thinking up a sharp response when I saw Jacob untie the thongs of his sandal and pry up the sole. There, neatly arranged between the sole and the leather lining, were a dozen silver coins.

"You had the money all along! What was in the pouch?"

"A rabbit's foot. Maybe it will bring them luck." Jacob chortled. "You know, those ruffians were only hungry. I don't think they meant to harm us for sport. Mattan, you must promise me that you won't let your temper get you into a fight again. You have a good head—think with it. Fighting's a fool's game. There will always be somebody bigger and stronger than you."

I was cross. "Just once, I want to be the biggest and strongest. After all, might makes right."

Jacob was quiet for a moment. "I am not so sure. It depends on what you think of as 'might.'" For the first time since I'd met him, Jacob spoke slowly, as if he was searching for each word. "That fellow Jesus? I think he will prove to be much stronger than the Romans."

"I don't understand. He doesn't have an army or soldiers. He wasn't carrying a sword. His followers don't carry weapons. What good are his words against swords and lances and horsemen?"

"We'll see, Mattan. Don't underestimate the power of ideas." He got to his feet. "For now, see how this idea sits with you: let's splurge on sleeping at an inn tonight."

Jacob was strangely quiet after that. He sighed with pleasure when the innkeeper's servant brought us hot water so that we could wash, but he hardly said a word. He took only a few bites of the innkeeper's delicious stew, so I finished it for him. I was too excited at the prospect of sleeping in an inn for the first time in my life to wonder if anything was troubling him.

The next morning was gray and drizzly, but Jacob was annoyingly cheerful. "I'm packing up, Mattan. I've decided to go back to Capernaum."

I sat up, rubbing my eyes. "Why would we go back there? Jesus is pulling in the crowds. We could keep going north, maybe as far as Syria. Imagine this: I could pretend to be mute and then, when you said a spell, I could burst out singing. People would go wild!"

"Mattan, I've been thinking all night. Maybe those bandits did me a favor. I'm too old to be on the road alone with a donkey and a boy."

I tried to protest, but he just went on. "Don't think I'm not grateful for the way you hopped into the fray yesterday, but we're bound to come across men who are more desperate and stronger."

"If you're afraid, Jacob, we could settle in a big town where people go to the market every day." I'd seen such markets with their stalls. "You know how to read and write. You could be a scribe, or a fortune-teller, or we could set up a stall and sell your potions."

"Mattan, there's something more. You may not understand. I can't say that I understand it myself. But when Peter told me how Jesus had healed—really healed—that woman, my heart went out of the swindle. A person can grow tired of trickery, and I am tired."

"You need a good rest, that's all." I noticed how Jacob's brown face had grown wrinkled and dry, like the ground when there has been no rain. "Why don't you stay here until you feel better? I'll take Devash and go on the road, and we'll come back for you. You tell me how long you need."

Jacob's smile was as sweet as ever. "You are growing up, Mattan. I thank you for the offer. But there's something pulling me toward Jesus. I liked the way his followers were like a family. I guess I'm lonely for family. Other than you and Devash, I have nobody. And then there are the words that Jesus said when he talked about the Kingdom of God and the life to come. I won't live forever. The idea of a better life after this one is a comfort. I have more to learn from him."

I didn't know what to say. There was plenty of drudgery in the way we lived, and I was certainly not making my fortune yet, but I'd grown to love the freedom, and Jacob's never-ending stories. He'd promised that we would go to Syria, where the great caravans of the world met. He guessed what I was thinking.

"You can go on," he said. "You've learned plenty of stories. You've proven you can take care of yourself. You can even have my basket of tonics."

I longed to do as he said, but the thought of Jacob's small figure heading back alone to Capernaum made me sick. "I'm probably going to regret this. I'm going with you."

Jacob bent over his pack so I couldn't see his face, but I heard him breathe a sigh of relief.

That's how we came to be followers of Jesus: Jacob because he believed and wanted to learn, and I because I wanted to be sure the crazy old fellow came to no harm. Besides, they would feed us.

Spring came, turning the desert a delicate green. We got to know Jesus' followers and the dozen or so men who were closest to him, his disciples. Among those disciples there were fishermen, farmers, scholars, and even a man who had once been a tax collector for the Romans. Together we moved from village to village. I watched Jesus heal a man who was raving and seeing things. He healed a leper. He even brought a dead man back to life. Amazing! It seemed like a miracle. I tried and tried to figure out how he did these things, but I just couldn't come up with an explanation.

Almost as puzzling to me were Jesus' stories. Everywhere he went, he used stories to teach people. At first I was baffled because the stories seemed so simple, or they didn't make sense. For example, Jesus told a tale about a farmer who sowed seeds. Some of the seeds fell on paving stones, some on rocky ground, some fell among thorns, and some on deep soil. Only the good soil yielded a good plant.

I snorted when I heard him tell it. "I figured that out when I was still a baby!"

Jacob shoved his pointy elbow into my ribs. "You are the son of a farmer. Try thinking about what he's saying! You may learn something." He muttered something that sounded like "mule head" under his breath. I wasn't going to let that pass.

That evening while we waded in a stream, I told Jacob that I thought maybe I had figured out the meaning. I was a bit nervous, and I hoped he'd tell me I had it right. I didn't want to be a "mule head."

"The seeds that fell on the paving stones didn't sprout at all because the birds flew off with the seeds. Maybe these are like the people who never get a chance to hear Jesus' message at all. The seeds on stony ground are like the people who hear what Jesus has to say about being kind but don't pay attention to what that really means. And the thorns—the thorns are like all the everyday things which clutter up our heads so that we lose the message. The last group, the deep soil, those are the people who not only listen but pay attention and let the new ideas grow inside them."

Jacob beamed at me. "Well, well, well! I'm proud of you, Mattan."

One day Jesus announced that he planned to go to Jerusalem for the festival of Passover. I was thrilled. Jerusalem was the city of my dreams. All my life I'd heard about the grand buildings, and the people who came there from all over, and the holy Temple where sacrifices were made to God. The Temple was the center of the Jewish world. I couldn't wait.

It turned out that I was the only one who was eager to go. The others argued with Jesus. After all, Roman authority was centered in Jerusalem. There would be no hiding in Jerusalem for anyone who opposed the Romans and their taxes.

Peter said to Jesus, "This is a terrible mistake. It is one thing to spread a message that challenges Rome when we are in faraway Galilee. It is quite another to stand right under the Romans' noses. Do you think they haven't heard things about you by now? Do you imagine they're going to welcome you with open arms? You could be arrested as a rebel. They might even execute you!" But nothing anybody said could change Jesus' mind.

We set out for Jerusalem together. No matter what they might have thought, the disciples were not going to let Jesus go alone.

When we arrived in the city, the first thing I did was climb the Mount of Olives to look out over the east wall of the Temple. The Romans may have been everywhere in Rome, but this was still our Temple. Every day, each Jew in the world turned toward the Temple to pray. The Temple was the house of God, at the very heart of the world. It was dazzling, covered all over with plates of gold. I counted its thirteen gates, stunned by how enormous it was.

Next I looked across the Temple to a building on the northwest corner of the Mount: the Antonia Fortress, named after Herod the Great's Roman patron, Mark Antony. It was smaller than the Temple. It was built not for God but for Romans. Roman soldiers patrolled the upper walls.

I had made it to Jerusalem! I was itching to explore the city. Here at last was where I would make my fortune. I was still concerned about Jacob and I wanted to keep an eye out for him, but he had become a favorite among the followers. I knew that they would care for him. Perhaps it would be all right for me to go. Maybe it was finally time for me to set out on my own.

I found my way back, through streets clogged with people, to the inn where we were staying. It was harder to say goodbye than I had thought it would be. Jesus was right when he said we were like a family. The others were seated around long tables in the inn's courtyard. I told them what I had in mind—how I wanted to find my own fortune, make my way in the world. Nobody tried to convince me to stay or to go, but each one had a kind, encouraging word to say to me. I had grown close to these earnest, devoted men and women.

I said goodbye to Jacob last. When I hugged him, I realized that I had grown a full head taller than him. I could feel his tears dampen my tunic. I tried not to cry.

"For once I have no words," he said. We both laughed. "God be with you." He pressed a few coins into my hand.

"And with you," I replied.

I stopped in at the stable to say goodbye to Devash. She bumped me gently with her head, as if to say she understood that I had to go.

Jerusalem during Passover was flooded with pilgrims to the Temple, not to mention all sorts of merchants hawking their wares, and an array of pickpockets, thieves, and beggars. In the marketplace I tried to take in the dazzling clash of hundreds of voices calling out in a dozen different languages, the brilliant colors of bolts of cloth for sale, the piles of yellow and orange spices. When I sniffed the delicious aroma of meat roasting at a kebab stand, I decided I was going to start my new life on a full stomach.

Before I could point to the skewer I wanted, a grubby hand reached around me and grabbed one from the brazier. The woman behind the stand shouted, "Stop, thief!" and took a few steps, but I could tell she would never catch the man. Without thinking, I pushed her aside and ran after him.

He dashed down a street that turned out to be a dead end, and I was able to grab him, the juicy skewer still in his hand. I realized that he was just a boy, younger than I was, and very frightened. I gripped his shaking arm, as thin as a bird's bone.

"You forgot to pay," I growled.

"Please, please. I was hungry," he muttered. He held the skewer between his teeth while he felt around in the bag that hung from his belt. Finally he admitted, "I have nothing."

I remembered the meals I'd shared with Jesus and his followers. "It's all right. Go! Just don't do it again."

When I got back to the kebab stand, I handed the woman one of Jacob's coins, cursing myself the whole time. Maybe I was too soft, but I didn't like the way I'd felt when I had the boy's trembling arm in my grip.

"God bless you! Thank you so much," said the woman. "You're a fine young man."

Not really, I thought, but I hung my head and tried to look humble.

She handed me a skewer of meat and said, "My last helper has vanished, and I have only two eyes." She insisted I take a second skewer, and before I had chewed the last mouthful I had a job with the widow Leah.

When she'd doused her charcoal fire and packed up the stand for the day, she asked me if I had a place to stay. I hesitated. "Come along, then. You can stay with us, if you don't mind sharing quarters with my old father and my children."

I started work the next day. I was surprised by how much I'd learned from Jacob. I knew how to convince a person to buy two kebabs when he didn't know he wanted even one. I could calculate change quickly. I had a knack for recognizing possible thieves. Soon the morning's kebabs had been sold. My head was spinning with ideas for a stall of my own.

Sometimes Leah had other kinds of chores for me. One day I had just returned from purchasing some spices for the kebabs when I saw her having an argument with a customer.

"What good is this to me?" Leah was shaking a coin in the man's face. "Can't you pay me in shekels?"

The man said something in Greek and then melted into the crowd.

Leah handed the foreign coin to me. "Mattan, go to the Temple and exchange this for shekels."

I wove through the crowded streets to the outer court of the Temple. With all the foreigners in town for Passover, there was a brisk business in exchanging foreign coins for our shekels—with a small profit to be made, of course. Other vendors were selling birds and animals to be offered as sacrifices. One way or another, there was a lot of money changing hands. The air was heavy and still, as if a storm were coming.

In one part of the courtyard I could see a large crowd gathered. I stood on a step, straining to see over all the heads, and I wasn't too surprised to discover that it was Jesus they were all there to listen to. I spotted Jacob and some of the other followers and squirmed through the mob so I could greet them and listen with them.

First somebody shouted a question. "Jesus, should taxes be paid to the Romans?"

Beside me, Jacob bristled. "That fellow's trying to set a trap. If Jesus says that the taxes should be paid, the mob will turn against him. But if he answers that taxes should not be paid, the Roman soldiers will arrest him on the spot."

Jesus paused for just a moment, as if weighing his choices, and then he asked somebody to hand him a coin. It was a silver denarius, engraved with a likeness of the Roman Emperor.

Jesus looked at the image of Tiberius on the coin. For a moment I wondered if he was going to do a coin trick, maybe make it disappear and then reappear out of thin air, the kind of thing Jacob used to do when he wanted to confuse his audience, but I dismissed the thought. Jesus held the coin out to the crowd. There was a hush as everyone waited, wondering, to hear how he would answer the question. The Roman soldiers were smiling smugly, looking for their opportunity to silence Jesus once and for all.

Jesus spoke calmly, explaining that because the Emperor's image was on the coin, it should be paid to the Emperor, and that everything that bore the image of God was God's.

Jacob dug his fingers into my arm. No one could have imagined such an answer.

It was clear that the Romans didn't understand what he meant—the soldiers were moving off now, apparently satisfied that the Emperor would be getting his taxes—but we Jews understood perfectly. The Torah says that human beings are made in the image of God. The message rang clear. The Romans could demand what they wanted, but our devotion, our loyalty, our duty, should be to God.

I didn't realize that I'd been holding my breath until I finally released it. I slumped with relief. I looked around for Jacob and the others, but the crowd had swept them away.

"We'll rest until the noon heat passes," said Leah.

It had been another busy morning at the kebab stall. Leah was supporting her elderly father and her children, so every shekel she earned was badly needed, but I could tell that she was more than happy with the business we had done so far that day. We enjoyed our break and sat in the shade of an awning with the young scribe who had the stall next to hers. She poured us all mint tea.

The scribe opened and closed his right fist to stretch out his stained fingers. He'd been writing letters and contracts all morning for pilgrims. "Don't get me wrong, I'm glad for all the extra work, but Passover can't come and go fast enough for me. I've never known Jerusalem to be at such a boil. Every day the Romans come through the market and arrest anyone they think might be stirring up rebellion. They look for rebels everywhere. I hate feeling that I'm being watched."

"I've met a rebel," I said, wanting to be part of the conversation. "A man called Jesus."

Leah looked at me curiously. "Jesus?"

"Yes. We're both from Nazareth, you know," I said, trying to sound important. "In fact, I'm one of his followers." I hadn't told Leah about seeing Jesus at the Temple, or about what I had been doing before I came to work for her. Why did she look so startled? Was it so surprising that I might know someone as important as Jesus was turning out to be?

"I heard Jesus teach once, when I went to Galilee to see my sisters. I will never forget it." She glanced around to see if anybody else was listening.

The scribe blew on his tea to cool it. "They say that he is so persuasive that if he were to call for us to arm ourselves and rise up against the Romans, we'd all do it, even though it would be suicide. I don't know about that, though. All I've heard him say is that if we follow the word of God today, our reward will come in the next life. That must be true, because we certainly aren't getting any rewards in this one."

"Even if you don't like the Romans, you've got to admit that they've built good roads," said the fruit seller who had the stall on the other side of Leah's. He wiped his hands and sweaty face with a rag, and sat under the awning with us.

"My father always complained that farmers had to pay hefty tolls to use the highways," I began, but Leah interrupted.

"Won't you have some tea?" She held a cup out to the fruit seller.

The man took a sip and continued. "It's those roads that let me wheel my cart of fresh fruit into the city without getting stuck in mud. That has to be worth something. They're turning us into a modern kingdom!"

"Maybe so, but you should hear Jesus talk about the Kingdom to come. It's much greater than anything the Romans could even imagine."

Leah and the scribe both tried to change the subject, but there was no stopping me.

"On our way to Jerusalem, Jesus told a story about a man who planted a vineyard. He built a wall around it and dug a cistern to catch the juice of the grapes, and he built a tower and rented it out to vine growers. Then he went away on a trip.

"When it was time to harvest, he sent a slave to the vine growers to collect some of the wine. The vine growers beat the slave and sent him away with nothing. The owner tried again, and again the slave was badly beaten. So the owner sent his son, his only son, because he thought that the vine growers wouldn't possibly hurt him. He was wrong: the vine growers killed his son. And of course the end of the story is that someday the owner will return and will destroy the evil vine growers and give the vineyard to someone who will deserve it." I looked at the others. "Does anyone get it?"

Leah and the scribe were busy staring at their tea, but I had the fruit seller's attention, so I went on. I thought I was getting pretty good at figuring out the meaning of Jesus' strange stories.

"What Jesus meant was that God is the one who owns the vineyard. The slaves they killed were the prophets whom God sends to show us the way. The vine growers didn't understand anything except violence. Jesus was telling us that the Kingdom of God will be taken away from violent people and given to people who won't act so horribly."

I saw an alarmed glance pass between Leah and the scribe. "Let's have no more talk of Jesus." Leah stood up and straightened her apron. "He's perfectly harmless with those childish stories of his."

When the noon sun was no longer burning overhead and the fruit seller saw buyers approaching his stand, he hurried back to work. And when she was sure he was out of earshot, Leah grabbed me roughly by the shoulders.

"You mustn't mention Jesus again." She shook me to make her point. "Do you understand? Weigh every word you say. Pilate, the Roman governor, is in Jerusalem for Passover. His spies are reporting on Jesus' followers and on the people who listen to Jesus preach and on anything they overhear people saying about him. That fruit seller could be one of the spies for all I know! But one thing is for sure, Jesus is only safe if they do not understand his message! And don't ask me how I know this!"

I felt my heart race. I tried to remember every word I'd said. Why, oh why, had I gone on about the hidden meaning of his stories? Had I betrayed anything about Jesus? I told myself that Jesus said what he believed, and he was saying it to more and more people, so it wasn't as though I was giving away any secrets, but that didn't make me feel any better.

I knew that there was no point in trying to warn Jesus. He understood exactly what he was doing and saying. Jesus would never stop speaking out. But what about Jacob and the rest of the followers? Maybe if I warned them, they could save themselves by leaving Jesus while there was still time.

The crooked street that led to the inn was lined with merchants selling carpets. Their wares hung above their stalls. I pushed past them blindly as I ran. A servant was sweeping the courtyard of the inn when I got there. Before I began looking for him, Jacob appeared. When I saw the wizened face that had become so dear to me, I started to cry. I couldn't help it.

"Come, boy, tell me why you're here."

"Jacob, I've been blabbing about Jesus' stories and what they really mean. Now people will know how he's criticizing the Romans and some of the priests too. What if they discover what he meant about the coin at the Temple? What if they turn on you all, because you follow Jesus? They'll kill you! Even if you can't change Jesus' mind, you can save yourselves."

"You do know that we will never leave him?" said Jacob gently.

That's when I started to sob.

For the first time since I'd met him, Jacob reached up and awkwardly stroked my hair. And before I could speak again, he said, "You should leave as quickly as you can. It's only a matter of time before they come for Jesus. We're not blind to his danger, or to our own."

It was clear there was nothing I could say that would convince Jacob to leave with me. It had never occurred to me that the danger they were all in was something *they* had understood all along, something that, to them, was just a part of the life they had chosen when they'd decided to follow Jesus.

"Where is Jesus now?"

"He and the disciples are eating dinner together. When they're finished, Jesus will go to the garden of Gethsemane to be alone and to pray."

Jacob wouldn't hear of me staying with him. He said I should go back to Leah and make sure she and her family were safe. Who knew what that fruit seller might have reported to the Romans?

I rushed back to Leah's home, and when I was sure she and her children and her elderly father were all safe for the night, I allowed myself to lie down to sleep. And as I lay there, listening to the sounds of a still-busy night market, I found myself thinking about strength—the strength of the Romans, but also the strength of Jesus and his followers. Theirs was the kind of strength that gave you the courage to do what you knew was right, even if it might lead to danger—even if it might end with your own death. Compared with that kind of strength, the brutish moneygrubbing of the Romans and their friends looked like nothing more than petty, childish bullying. That wasn't really strength, I thought—not the kind that mattered.

Leah shook me awake. "The Romans have arrested Jesus." There were tears in her eyes.

I thought I was prepared for such awful news, but I was not.

I felt faint. With trembling fingers, I dressed. I had to be with the followers.

A few hours later, I stood shivering in the morning chill in the midst of a noisy crowd that had gathered near the fortress. I'd heard what happened. One of his own disciples had betrayed Jesus to the Romans. We knew that Jesus' fate was now in the hands of Pilate, the Roman governor of Judea. When he emerged from the fortress to speak to the gathered crowd, we expected news, but he told us nothing of Jesus. He wouldn't even mention him. It was as though he had simply disappeared, as though he didn't even matter.

"What's going to happen to Jesus?" I asked Jacob over and over.

His voice trembled when he spoke. "We're not sure what charge they've arrested him on, but it could be treason, sedition, rebelling against the authority of Rome. Pilate is not the wisest person at the best of times. In a case like this, he's more likely to execute a prisoner outright than waste time with a proper trial. If Jesus is lucky, they'll drive a sword through him and kill him on the spot. If he's not, they will nail his hands and feet to a cross and leave him to die. It's horribly cruel, but that's what they do to anyone who dares to speak against Rome."

I couldn't believe it had come to this, that Jesus might be put to death just for speaking his simple truths. Looking at the grief on Jacob's face, I felt a sob rise into my throat, and when Jacob put his arms around me, we both wept.

"Jacob," I said, "this can't be the end."

When Jacob spoke again, his voice was firmer, steadier somehow, as though he had dug down deep within himself looking for strength.

"It won't be, Mattan. We have Jesus' words in our hearts. He has taught us well. We will always have that, no matter what they do."

I pieced together the rest of the story from various people's accounts. After Jesus was put to death on the cross, the followers scattered in different directions—to Syria, to Egypt, to the east. Nowhere the Romans ruled was really safe for them, because of their association with Jesus. But they needed to tell his story, share the ideas that they had learned from him, keep his message alive. They spread it everywhere they went.

Later I found out that Jacob had gone to Rome. I hear they have great magicians there. Sometimes I wonder if he's taken up trickery again.

As for me, I brought Devash home with me to Nazareth— a gift from Jacob.

I didn't go home a hero, at least not the kind of hero I'd imagined. Somewhere on the road, the boy who had once run away from sorrow and hard work had vanished. I wasn't ashamed anymore that we were the poor, the meek, the humble. Jesus had taught me that we were all important in God's eyes, even if the Romans didn't think so. I'd learned that even if life is hard, if we act honorably toward others, we will be rewarded in the life to come.

I thought about that last day with Nirit. If I hadn't stayed behind to watch the Romans, she wouldn't have been hurt, and she wouldn't have died. Even if my family didn't blame me, it didn't matter: I blamed myself enough. But I was finished using my grief and guilt as an excuse for doing what I wanted to do, for acting selfishly. I was ready to help my family face our troubles. And, like the disciples, I would talk about what Jesus had taught me for the rest of my life.

I got home just as the sun was setting. Shua, much slower than she used to be, barked a greeting. She and Devash nosed each other suspiciously. Father, his hair and beard whiter, came out of the house. I hung back for a moment, afraid he would still be angry that I'd left, but his arms were open wide.

"Welcome home, dear Mattan. Your brothers will be glad of another pair of hands," he said. I bent my knee so that he could place his hands on my head to bless me.

Mother was arranging sweet-smelling herbs in a jar. When she heard me come in, she clapped her hands to her mouth. She kissed me, wiped her eyes, and ordered me to wash my face and feet to make myself presentable for the Sabbath.

EPILOGUE

Jesus predicted that he would die to pay for the sins of mankind, but that he would rise again. After his crucifixion, the disciples buried him in a tomb. Those who had condemned him to death knew that he'd predicted his resurrection, so they put guards around his tomb and sealed it with a heavy stone.

When the followers went to the tomb a few days later, they found it empty. They reported that an angel had met them and told them that Jesus was no longer there, that he had risen.

At first, only his Jewish disciples followed Jesus' teachings, but those disciples, the apostles, carried his message with them to the rest of the Roman Empire and beyond. Among the disciples were those who wrote down the words Jesus had said, and who wrote letters to one another. These writings are collected in the Christian New Testament.

FALLAH

"Are they coming?"

"Yes. As sure as night follows day." My mother clutched me against her.

The walls of our tent snapped and groaned in the wind. The desert could be cold at night, but it was the sound of the camels' pounding hoofbeats that made us shiver. I had spent the long day crowded in the tent with my aunts and small cousins, waiting for the battle to come.

At the last full moon, a band of our tribesmen—my father included—had stolen five camels from another tribe. Worse, much worse, my father had killed a member of the other tribe. He hadn't meant to—nobody wanted to kill during a raid, because of what would follow. Now it was the full moon again and that death would have to be avenged. A man from that tribe would have to kill my father. And then my father's eldest son, my brother Zayed, would have to kill that killer, and on and on and on. That was the rule of the blood feud: if a member of one tribe injured or killed a person in another tribe, then the injured tribe had the right—the duty—to seek vengeance. Nobody could remember a time when things were different.

I could hear the thunder of hooves as the riders approached. "I'm so frightened for Father."

If Mother answered me, her voice was lost in the din of war cries. For a time the air rang with the shrieking of the camels and the clash of steel against steel. Then it was over. The only sounds were the sighing of the wind and the tent straining against its ropes.

"I want to see what's happened."

My mother held me back. "No, Fallah. Zayed will tell us soon enough," she said. Her calmness was unsettling.

My older brother Zayed pushed aside the leather tent flap. I could smell sweat and fresh blood—the smell of battle—on him. He was fifteen, and this was the first time he had fought among the men.

"Father is dead," he said, and sobbed in my mother's arms.

My uncles helped Zayed and me to dig Father's grave. After we buried him, I placed a small stone on the grave to mark its place. Someone had rigged up an awning to give us shade so we could sit by the grave, mourning.

My mother came out of the tent carrying cups of camel milk. My uncle reached for one with a bandaged hand.

He said, "It is your turn now, Zayed. The next kill will be yours to do. It is a question of honor."

Zayed mumbled, "I suppose so."

My mother became still for a moment. I thought she might speak, but she said nothing.

That night, the women sat together in the tent, weeping. The wind was fierce, howling. I lay on my pallet and remembered my father's voice lulling me to sleep as he recited a poem about a brave tribesman lost in a desert storm. I thought I was dreaming when I felt my mother's hand squeezing my shoulder.

"Wake up, my son," she whispered.

It was hard to see in the gloom of the tent, but I could tell Zayed was with her.

"I want you both to go."

"Go?" I repeated. "I don't understand."

"I will stand for no more killing. Zayed will kill and be killed, and then it will be your turn to seek vengeance. I have had enough! Surely this cannot be why we are on this earth?" There was steel in her voice.

"But Father's honor—" Zayed began.

"Honor ends at the grave. I want more for my children than a sudden, useless death. I want you to leave here and never come back."

"This is a terrible thing you are asking!" Zayed was close to tears. "We will belong nowhere if we leave the tribe!"

The tribe was everything to us. Together, we cared for our goats and sheep. Together, we crossed the vast and brutal desert to find pasture for our small herds. Together, under the brilliant starry night sky, we shared ancient stories. The tribe was our family, our past, our protection. Living outside the tribe was something neither of us could imagine. We would be nameless, as puny as single grains of sand in the desert.

"We can't leave you!" I said. "What will happen to you, now that Father's gone?"

"Don't worry about me. Now that I am a widow, your father's brother has to take care of me. I will tell everyone that I tried to stop you but you ran off together tonight to take your revenge on your father's killer, and you were lost in the sandstorm. I am prepared to live without you as long as I know that you feel the same sun on your face as I do, and that you look up at the sky and see the same stars."

My mother always measured every word she spoke. We knew there was no arguing with her. She had put together packs for us—some dried fruit, some nuts, some mare's cheese, and skins of water—and kissed us goodbye.

The wind was shrieking as we pulled aside the flap of the tent. We were bent almost double as we headed away from our tribe's camp, and the driving sand battered our skin. But nothing in that wild night was as frightening as the idea of being on our own for the first time in our lives, with no family, no tribe to belong to.

We fought the wind and sand as we trudged through that long, cold night, trying to get as far away as we could. At daybreak we found a cave to shelter in. We climbed inside, took a few sips of water, and fell to the rocky ground, exhausted.

We must have slept all day, because the sun was setting when we woke. I looked out and saw, near the mouth of the cave, a petrified tree. It was dry and old and twisted, as hard and dead as rock.

"Look, Zayed, that must be the home of a *jinn*."

The desert was full of spirits—jinns. I knew lots of places

that had such spirits: springs where the water gurgled and spoke to me, or stones, or trees like this one.

"I wonder if the jinn in the tree is a kind spirit or an evil one." You could never tell how a jinn would behave.

"For our sake, it had better be one of the kind ones. Now, try to sleep, Fallah."

Many days passed—we lost track of time—while we hid from our tribesmen in that cave. We hardly spoke to each other. We took turns sleeping so one of us was awake to watch for hyenas or wolves in the night. While Zayed slept, I recited long poems about lone travelers who survived the hardships of the desert. When I'd run through the ones I knew, I tried to compose one, but that was much harder.

We tried to make our food last, but eventually the night came when the sun set and we were still painfully hungry. I tried to sleep while Zayed kept watch. When I woke, I was hungrier than ever.

"Zayed, we have to leave here or we'll starve." I felt desperate.

He didn't answer me. He just grunted, rolled over, and slept.

I sat cross-legged at the mouth of the cave, staring at the petrified tree, until the sun finally set. I talked to the jinn, asking if I would live to see it rise again.

Then, against the bright night sky, I saw a beautiful sight. A plume of smoke rose from behind the wall of rocks that hid our cave. It wasn't the smoke that finally woke Zayed, though. It was the smell of cooking fires.

We waited hungrily until the night grew darker. Then we scrambled down the rocky slope into the valley below, in the direction of the smoke.

We came upon a caravan—a rich merchant's, by the size of it. There were a few goat-hair tents huddled together, and dozens of camels tethered for the night. Guards stood by piles of what looked like bolts of cloth.

Men were seated by a fire in front of the tents, talking and laughing and enjoying what was left of their dinner.

There was another cooking fire closer to where we were hiding. We crept up to it. Some meat was still turning on a spit. I was so hungry I couldn't stop myself from reaching out to tear off a handful. But the flames burned me and I yelped. The next thing I knew, I was dangling in the air.

"Caught you, you thieving hyenas!"

A tall, powerful man, his braided beard and hair laced with gray, held Zayed in one hand and me in the other. He dropped us, and I thought about running away, but the smell of roasting lamb stopped me.

"What is your tribe? Whom do you belong to?"

I was afraid to speak. What if he had heard of our father's death, and knew that we'd run away from our duty? What if he thought we had not loved our father enough to avenge his death?

"Surely you must know your own tribe!" he said. Then, less gruffly, "It doesn't matter. You must be bedouins, to have survived in the desert on your own. Are you hungry?"

I said nothing. My stomach gave me away—it growled. The man laughed and called out, "Qasim, my son, see that these boys get something to eat."

Qasim was a boy not much older than me, about thirteen, and I could tell he was proud that he'd been put in charge of us. Soon we were sitting among the camel boys, wrapping hunks of warm bread around shreds of meat and stuffing them into our famished mouths.

Qasim liked to talk. "That man you met is my father, Walid. We are members of the Hashim clan." Again came the question I dreaded. "Where do you belong?" he asked.

We didn't have to think of an answer because Qasim turned away just then to settle a squabble between two of the camel boys.

After we had eaten, Qasim took us to his father. Walid was telling a story.

"Once there were seven small boys and their faithful sheepdog, you see. Some Romans found them praying to God. They weren't praying to Roman gods, and that made the Romans furious, so they walled the boys up in a cave and left them to die. But a miracle happened. Because they believed in their God, they didn't die, they just fell asleep, and woke two hundred years later. So you see, even the very weakest can find favor if he has faith."

Walid motioned for us to come near. Perhaps the jinn in the tree really was a kind spirit. Or maybe Walid was just a kind man. In any case, he saved us: he told us that the caravan had room for two more camel boys until we got to the city of Mecca. Then we would be on our own. When we tried to thank him, he waved our words away.

"I believe you bedouin have a way with camels. Prove to me that I am right."

Zayed and I had heard stories about the wonders of Mecca— its throngs of people, its marketplaces, and of course its sacred places—but we were too busy to think much about what we would do once we were there. All day, we walked beside the heavily laden camels, helping keep them in line. At nightfall, we took the camels' heavy loads of silk and cloth and leather from their backs and fed and watered them. The camels rested, but we didn't. We gathered their droppings for cooking fuel, and though by that time we were exhausted, we were still not done. Many nights we stayed up to guard the caravan against wolves and mountain lions.

The last day of the trek to Mecca dawned hot and windy. Everyone was eager for the long journey to end. I found Zayed, his face shining with sweat, trying to make one of the camels get to his feet.

"What's wrong, Brother? We're ready to go. The merchants are getting impatient."

"This wretched camel refuses to budge!" He prodded the animal. That didn't work. Camels could be foul creatures, some of them. Many times I'd wiped camel spit from my face.

Zayed tried yelling at the camel. It looked at him calmly from under its feathery eyelashes. The other camel boys were hooting with laughter.

I didn't want to shame Zayed, but I had a way with these stubborn beasts. I took the rope from my brother and gave it just the right tug. If you jerked too hard, the camel would balk. Quietly, I clicked my tongue. I tugged again, clicked again, and the camel finally got up.

That last, long day's trek finally ended as the sun was setting. We paused on a cliff and looked down the narrow, rocky valley at the city of Mecca, hemmed in on all sides by mountains. It was hard to make out the buildings through the smoke of hundreds of cooking fires. The mountains that surrounded Mecca felt as though they were walling me in, as if I were one of the sleeping shepherd boys in the cave in Walid's story.

"Zayed, why would anyone pick such a place to live?"

"Water, I suppose," he replied. "There's a spring here."

I watched vultures reel in the sky at the edge of the town. Zayed answered before I could ask. "That must be the dung heap."

We followed Qasim and the others down a stony road into the city. Once we had unloaded the camels and stabled them, Qasim gave us each a few coins. "My father says this is your pay."

The other camel boys were heading down one of the narrow streets. We didn't know what else to do, so we followed them. I felt as if I were in a sandstorm, but one made of harsh noises and glaring colors and sharp smells. I'd never imagined there were so many people in the whole world, and now they all seemed to be here, moving in all directions at once. I took Zayed's hand, but he was as lost as I was.

I had to crane my neck to see the sky above me; it was almost hidden by balconies jutting out from the houses, strung with drying clothes and sleeping mats.

And then we came into the light. We reached an open space around a simple granite building.

"Look, Fallah," Zayed said quietly. "That must be it, the Kaaba."

The Kaaba was a holy place. I had heard my father describe it so many times that I felt I had been here before. Something about the building filled me with awe. The roof was constructed of palm fronds draped with cloth. In a circle around the Kaaba were symbols of all the gods: the god of love and friendship, the god of weather, the moon-god, the god of war, and many others. Some of the symbols were small, smooth stones, and others were taller than the tallest man I'd ever seen. Somebody had put garlands on one or two of them, maybe in thanks for prayers answered. The Kaaba was so sacred that hardly anyone was permitted inside, but people claimed it held all kinds of treasures, or maybe weapons. I liked to think it was empty, full of spirits you couldn't see.

With the others, and like the men of our tribe who had come before us, we performed the ritual of circling the Kaaba seven times, our left shoulders toward the building. I could never explain it, but as we walked in silence, all the sorrow I'd felt ever since the raid that killed my father and the awful time in the cave drained away from me for the moment, and I no longer felt so lost. Zayed's eyes were closed and I could see an unfamiliar peace in his face.

The other boys drifted away. Just beyond the Kaaba was a busy street lined with stalls. I tried to make sense of all the hubbub. There were scribes writing letters for people, fruit vendors, carts piled high with spices, and poets reciting. I stopped in front of a stall where a man was sitting on a stool with a group of people seated on the ground around him. His voice was beautiful as he recited.

"I know this poem, Zayed! Do you remember it?"

The poet, a round man with skin as smooth and shiny as a ripe olive, was reciting a poem about a desperate battle fought long ago among the stars in the sky. Zayed blinked back tears at the familiar words. My father had taught me that poem.

The poet's voice grew scratchy and finally it broke. He pounded his chest and coughed. A tiny woman—his wife, I was to learn—handed him a cup of water. While he sipped it, I couldn't help myself: I took up the words where he'd left off.

Zayed elbowed me to be quiet, but the poet just smiled. He motioned that I should join him. I stepped through the bystanders, faced them, and started to recite.

When I was finished, many of the listeners dropped coins into the poet's clay jar. He asked me my name.

"Fallah, sir." I braced myself for the inevitable question about my tribe, but it didn't come.

"And I am Omar. Boy, someone taught you well." I made no reply, so he went on. "Are you new here? I've not seen you before. Come, come, don't be frightened, child."

The listeners were growing impatient. Somebody called out the name of a poem and Omar began to recite again.

Zayed tugged at my arm. "Come on, Fallah. Let's go."

We wandered, amazed, among the bolts of silk, the musicians, and the food vendors, until darkness fell.

That first night, with no idea where else to go, we slipped down a narrow alleyway where we couldn't be seen and I sat on the ground, leaning against the wall of a house.

Zayed slumped down wearily beside me. "How are we ever going to survive in this place, Fallah?" he asked. "All we have are the coins Walid gave us. We should never have left home."

I was just as tired as Zayed, but not as discouraged.

"Sleep now," I told him. "I have an idea."

The next morning, Zayed followed me back to the poet Omar's stall.

"Please, sir, do you have work for me?"

I thought Omar was about to say no when his wife clucked at him and crossed her arms.

"All right, all right, woman!" He flapped his hand at her. "As you can tell, I have too little breath left in me to recite much. I am a *sha'ir*—I write poems—but often I can't recite them. The cough has robbed me of that gift. I have a mind to let you be my *rawi*, my reciter."

Omar's wife smiled.

Zayed whooped. He stepped in front of me. "You won't be sorry. My brother may be small, but his voice is the purest in all of Arabia! Recite some more, Fallah!"

I looked at Omar and he nodded encouragement. "Let me hear what you can do."

I recited a short poem about the sand dunes in the desert as carefully as I could, so that the rhythm made me sound almost as if I were singing.

When I was finished, Omar's wife clapped her hands. "Fallah! Your reciting is wonderful! You should enter the poetry contest that will be held during the hajj."

I was thrilled about the contest, and about the hajj. My father and one of my uncles had once made the journey to Mecca to take part, as had my grandfather, and his grandfather. People had been coming to Mecca on an annual pilgrimage for hundreds and hundreds of years, to circle the Kaaba and to make an animal sacrifice. It had all begun when our ancestor Abraham sent his son Ishmael and Ishmael's mother, Hagar, into the desert. When they had nothing left to drink, an angel touched down to earth and showed Hagar where to find water. The Kaaba marked the place where she found the sweet, fresh spring that kept her and her baby alive.

"And the winner will have his name carved into the walls of the Kaaba," Omar's wife went on. "You could enter the contest and win a sack of silver."

Omar fished a coin from his jar. "You've earned this, boy. Go find yourself something to eat, and something for your brother too. You will start this afternoon."

I bought us pistachio cakes oozing with honey and we sat down to savor them.

"Did you hear what that woman said, Zayed? Imagine! If I won the poetry contest, we could buy a camel, and even have our own caravan. This has all been so easy!"

Zayed's mouth was full of sweet cake, so I didn't catch his answer.

We may have been fatherless, but I felt as though Father was still protecting us. The poetry my father had given me was his gift. I felt that he was watching over us in this strange place.

We washed at the public baths before heading to Omar's stall. As we were making our way back, we heard a commotion.

A man in a simple, threadbare robe was walking down the street that led to the Kaaba. People were taunting and swearing at him. One boy threw a fistful of thorns in his path. Others threw chunks of dirt and rotten fruits and vegetables at him. All the while, the man's expression was calm and determined. He didn't even flinch.

We hurried to Omar's stall. "What has that man done?" I asked.

"His name is Muhammad. It is shameful, how they make him suffer! Once, when he was praying at the Kaaba, somebody even threw a sheet around his neck, jerked it, and made him fall on his face. You can't live in Mecca without knowing about him. Come, it's still early. Bring me some tea, wife, and I will tell the boys about him before the paying customers come."

We settled under the palm fronds that shaded Omar's stall, and he began.

"I am honored to tell you his story. Muhammad is a member of the Hashim clan, as am I. He is fatherless," began Omar.

"So are we," I interrupted.

"Hmm. I thought so," Omar murmured. "So you understand that particular hardship. Well, when Muhammad's father died, his mother was left with almost nothing, only five camels and a slave girl. The mothers of Mecca often send their babies out of the city's foul air, away from the city's diseases, to live with foster parents in the desert, and that's what happened to Muhammad. His first sights and sounds were of the desert, the bleating of sheep and the sighing of the always-blowing wind—as were yours, I suppose.

"When he was three, he was returned to his mother, but she died soon after. Muhammad then went to live with his grandfather, who also soon died. Once again the boy was passed to another home. This time he was sent to live in the household of his uncle Abu Talib, who had become the chief of the Hashim clan and a person of some importance.

"Abu Talib and Muhammad's other uncles made sure that he could shoot an arrow, handle a sword, and wrestle. They taught him to be a good merchant and took him on caravans to Syria and Mesopotamia. But still, in everyone's eyes, he was nothing but an orphan. With no father to tie him to his clan, he was unanchored, alone, an outsider."

I listened intently. I was beginning to understand what that felt like, and it was frightening, and lonely.

"Nevertheless, everybody respected Muhammad as a fair person. Years ago, a trader from Yemen was robbed in Mecca. His cries for help were ignored. The trader was so angry that he wrote a poem mocking the heartless Meccans and he read it aloud in a public square. One of Muhammad's uncles heard him, and he felt so ashamed that he called the city elders together to form a group called Hilf al-Fudul to protect people, including foreigners. Though he was young, Muhammad became a member of Hilf al-Fudul, pledging to take care of others, especially those who were weaker. Many years later, Muhammad talked about that pledge. He said, 'I am not prepared to break my promise even against a herd of camels. If somebody should appeal to me even today, by virtue of that pledge, I would hurry to his aid.'

"In fact, he played an important role once in solving a tricky situation. Some years ago, as you might know, the Kaaba caught fire and burned to the ground. All the tribes of Mecca took part in repairing it. But when all the work was done, they had a dilemma. The question was, what should be done with the Black Stone?"

"The Black Stone?"

"Yes. It is part of the Kaaba's wall and it's very ancient. They say that it comes from the time of Adam and Eve, from long before even Abraham and Moses. Well, when it came time to put the Black Stone back in its place, each of the four leading families in Mecca claimed the honor should be theirs. How would they solve the problem? They appealed to Muhammad, and he came up with a clever solution. He spread a white sheet on the ground and placed the stone in its center. Then he told the elders of each clan to lift a corner of the sheet and carry it to its site. Finally, with his own hands, he put the stone in place. All of the families carried the stone, and that way he preserved everyone's honor!"

"So . . . what happened to make people turn on him?" asked Zayed.

"The torment started a few years ago. Like other *hanif*, pious men, during the month of Ramadan, Muhammad went up to a cave in the mountains to think and pray. Then a miracle happened." Omar's face lit up as he continued. "An angel in human form appeared to Muhammad. 'Read!' commanded the angel.

"Muhammad replied that he didn't know how. The angel gripped him by the shoulders, and right there, he taught him. And after that, the words of Allah poured out of Muhammad's mouth."

"What did Muhammad do? Was he scared? I'd have been scared!" I said.

Omar spoke softly, caught up in the wonder of the story. "He was confused, and I suppose he was terrified. Who wouldn't be? He ran down from the mountain to his wife, Khadijah. When he burst into the house, he cried that he had been cursed. He said a jinn, a spirit, had told him to recite some texts he could not read. He had seen lights and heard sounds and felt he was being crushed. He begged her to tell him: was he losing his mind?

"Khadijah calmed him. She took him to a seer, who could tell them about the future. 'This is only the beginning,' said the seer, after Muhammad told him what had happened. 'There are more revelations to come.'

"And the revelations from Allah did keep coming. Muhammad couldn't make them come or stop them from coming. Over the years, they came to him when he was praying, but also when he was speaking, and even when he was out riding his camel. You could tell when it was happening: his face would turn red and soon he'd be drenched in sweat, even when it was cold.

"This seer told Muhammad that he was to be the prophet of his people. But he had a warning: not everybody would want to hear what Muhammad had to say. And that prophecy has certainly come true. You have seen it yourself."

"Have you heard his revelations?" I wanted to know.

"I have." Omar unscrewed a small vial that hung from a golden chain around his neck. He pulled out a rolled scrap of thin leather and gently smoothed it with a fingertip. "At first, Muhammad would memorize Allah's revelations and repeat them only to his family and friends, but eventually he told them to anybody who would listen. We wrote them down. This is one."

I reached out to touch it.

"Careful! It is the most precious thing I own."

"What does it say?"

"The words are beautiful. They speak of the life to come, and how our good deeds will be rewarded then."

"But I still don't understand why Muhammad is taunted in the street. Do they think he made the whole story up?"

"No, boy, it's not that. They believe him. But ever since Muhammad started to speak of his revelation, the message of Allah has spread, and that is making the Quraysh furious."

This made no sense to me. "Why should that be?"

"Well, that's harder to explain, but think of it this way. The Quraysh are the most powerful tribe in Mecca. They control access to the spring that is Mecca's lifeblood. Without a source of water in the desert, nothing could survive here—there would be no Mecca. They alone are allowed to decide who enters the Kaaba to clean it—they hold on to all its secrets. And during the hajj, they charge pilgrims outrageous prices for food and housing and put taxes on just about anything you can name. Put that all together—the water, who can enter the Kaaba when it is cleaned, and the trade—and you will understand why the Quraysh are so powerful."

"But what has that got to do with Muhammad?"

"Well, Muslims—that means those of us who submit to the will of God—believe that there is no God but Allah, and that Muhammad is God's messenger. And the message?" He paused. "Muhammad says that everybody has equal value—everybody— no matter what tribe they belong to. He has been speaking out against corruption and calling for justice for all, rich and poor alike. Can you imagine? And he tells us there is one God, not the many gods the Quraysh worship."

I had never heard anybody say such a thing. Fatherless, tribeless people like Zayed and me having the same worth as the richest man in Mecca?

Omar seemed to read my mind. "Let me tell you, I was not easily convinced, but Muhammad is very persuasive. He has a following in Mecca, and it's getting bigger all the time—too big for the Quraysh to ignore. He says that people who aren't even related to one another should join together and put aside past feuds. The poor and rich, men and women, orphans and slaves—we all have merit if we submit to Allah. We are a clan made up of people who aren't even members of the same family. We call ourselves Companions.

"But these are matters for you to judge for yourself. Now, suck on this piece of honey candy. It will sweeten your voice for the customers."

As the days passed, I became used to life in Mecca. I still longed for my mother and the clear, open sky that I could hardly see in the smoky city, but as I got to know the other stall-keepers near the Kaaba precinct, I began to feel less strange. With Omar by my side, I recited the poems I had learned from my father and new ones that he taught me. Omar's wife fussed over me to make sure I washed and ate well.

I hardly ever saw Zayed, except at night when he shared the narrow pallet that was my bed in Omar's stall. He was growing more and more gloomy. Making a life in Mecca was much harder for him. He couldn't find work. But when I tried to talk to him, he always cut me off.

"In this world, you need connections, Fallah. Everybody else here has a cousin or an uncle who helps them get work. Face it, I am nothing in this place. Nothing but a coward too afraid to kill for my father's honor."

There was no use arguing. I had been in Mecca long enough to know that much of what he said was true. Mecca was like a cloth, and every person was a thread in it, connected somehow to every other person. Except us. We didn't have a father, or a clan, and we were on our own. It galled Zayed that he had to rely on me for food.

One morning, I was peeling an orange for Omar while he recited when Zayed shouldered through the audience around the stall. He was grinning.

"I have news, Brother. I've found work," he said. "I was passing a house when the gate flew open and out ran a man covered in flour, swearing that he wouldn't work another moment for such a wicked master. I thought to myself, *I've survived in the desert. I can surely survive any master.* So I asked to see the head of the kitchen servants, and he took me on right away. I have a job! I help the cook in the kitchen."

When Omar finished the poem, he congratulated Zayed. "Who is this master?" he asked. "Do you know his name?"

"It's Abu l'Hakam."

Omar raised his eyebrows. I could tell he wanted to say something more.

"The cook told me that Abu l'Hakam is a big man in the Quraysh tribe," Zayed went on. "And that's as high as you can get around here," he said proudly. "The most powerful tribe in Mecca, and I work for the most powerful man in it!"

After Zayed left to start his new job, I asked Omar about Abu l'Hakam.

He sighed. "Abu l'Hakam is a man I fear. He has brought together the city leaders to smear Muhammad's good name. They call the Prophet a liar, and worse. They claim that he has been tricked by a jinn, or possessed by a demon. They say anything they can think of that will turn people against him. All of us Companions fear him."

I was happy that Zayed had found work, but I felt a prickle of fear. A powerful man who would launch a campaign to smear the reputation of another—what kind of man was Abu l'Hakam?

The air in Mecca seemed to crackle with excitement as the hajj approached. I seldom saw Zayed now. Abu l'Hakam was keeping him busy cooking for the guests who would come to his home from as far away as Syria and Egypt.

One night, Omar asked me if I wanted to come with him and his wife to hear Muhammad myself. I was curious, and agreed. We carried no torch to light our way because the location was a secret one.

"We always meet in different people's houses, for safety," Omar explained. "The Quraysh have spies everywhere. We can't take any chances."

We had to duck to enter the tiny room where people had gathered. I looked at the rapt faces around me: slaves, women, two or three people my age wearing heavy gold rings, and then—Walid. Walid, the merchant who had been so good to Zayed and me in the desert. So he was a Companion! I didn't think he would recognize me as the starving, grubby boy who had helped tend his camels.

Silence fell. Muhammad rose and faced us. He was neither tall nor short, with broad shoulders, curly hair starting to gray, and a thick beard. He didn't look remarkable, but once he started to speak, he was transformed. In words that sounded like poetry, Muhammad preached that everybody should worship only one God, Allah, not other gods or jinn. He talked about how, after we died, we would be measured by the good we had done, and not by how much money we had made. If we did good in the world, we would spend eternity in Paradise, a place of indescribable delights.

He talked about how we were all one people, and how the tribal differences that separated us were trifles compared with the many ways we all belonged together as brothers and sisters. When he said that we had to put an end to blood feuds,

I almost started to cry. I thought of our mother's words on the night she sent us away to save us from dying a cruel death for a cruel custom. It made me think that she would have liked what Muhammad said.

When Muhammad finished, Omar left me to make my own way back to the stall in the dark. I could hardly believe what I had seen—all those people from different families, listening together in peace. Still, what Muhammad was asking of his followers was to give up believing in all the familiar gods that had always been part of our lives. I had lost so much already . . . I wasn't sure I wanted to lose that comfort as well.

I spent the next day practicing the poem I was to recite at the contest during the hajj. It was one of my father's favorites, about the light of a hermit's lamp showing the way to a solitary traveler in the desert. When I felt it was ready at last, I recited it for Omar. But thinking about the desert made me so homesick that I lost my place, and I swore.

Omar patted my shoulder. "I say this simply to rest your voice, Fallah—perhaps you should visit Zayed. Now's the time to go. We'll be busy from dawn to midnight once the visitors begin arriving."

I wiped my face with my hands and thanked him.

Abu l'Hakam's kitchen was a small building off the courtyard of his fine stone house. By then it was evening, and Zayed and I climbed to the flat roof to shell walnuts by the light of a lantern. Abu l'Hakam was entertaining a group of traders from far-off Syria and Lebanon who had come for the hajj. We could hear him barking an order below us.

"So that's your master," I said. "The great Abu l'Hakam."

Zayed shrugged. "When he gets like this, I just try to be invisible and imagine I'm riding free across the desert. Let me tell you, I think about the desert a lot." He laughed.

The courtyard below was lovely. An incense burner perfumed the air. A songbird trilled sweetly in a lemon tree. Silent women moved gracefully among the seated men, passing silver trays of dried apricots and skewers of meat. It was like an oasis, fragrant and serene. But then one of the Syrians asked about Muhammad in admiring tones.

"I would like to learn more about this Muhammad. I hear he claims to be the prophet of Allah," he said. "Quite a claim for a man they say lives simply. My good wife tells me he sews his own clothes, mends his own sandals, waters the camels, milks the goats, and even does the marketing. Is it true that he has only one set of clothes, and these he washes himself? Isn't it wonderful that Allah's words pour from the mouth of such a modest man!"

Though he tried to keep his voice even, I could tell that Abu l'Hakam was enraged.

"Friends, when I first heard what Muhammad was saying, I laughed at his wild ideas. After all, he claims that his words come directly from his one true God. The words are elegant, to be sure, but can you imagine Allah sending his messages through a simple man like Muhammad, who can neither read nor write? It's ludicrous! He must have paid someone to write them.

"But now he is going too far. It's not a laughing matter anymore. Let us take the business of slaves. How dare Muhammad question what a master can do to a slave? It is bad enough that Muhammad thinks of slaves as human beings. Everyone knows that they are not our brothers. Slaves are property, like the carpet on which we sit!"

Abu l'Hakam paused to offer dates and coffee to the others.

He turned to one of the guests—a richly robed merchant from Mecca. "Do you not agree, my friend?"

"Of course! I know Muhammad as a good and honest businessman, but as for all this prophecy . . . well, that's nonsense. The gods of health and the gods of prosperity have smiled on us, have they not, friends? I see no reason to abandon them." He chuckled.

"Never mind," said Abu l'Hakam. "Somehow, I suspect that Muhammad will soon have reason to wish he had never caused all this turmoil. As for his friends, the Companions—we know who they are—they will wish they had never listened to a word he's spoken."

Beside me, Zayed was nodding as Abu l'Hakam spoke. "He's right about Muhammad. Muhammad wants people to abandon the ways of their fathers."

"We did," I said as mildly as I could.

Zayed slammed down his hand, making the walnuts dance in the bowl. "Muhammad is a troublemaker. I don't want you to go near him. Do you understand? Trouble is coming—real trouble—to him and his Companions. I hear Abu l'Hakam and the other heads of the Quraysh making plans. Stay away from Muhammad. Promise me, Fallah!"

I didn't want to tell Zayed that Omar was a Companion. I just mumbled, "I'll be careful."

That satisfied Zayed. We went back to shelling walnuts, and to help pass the time while we worked, he asked me to recite a poem.

I chose one of our old favorites from home, a poem about how an abandoned campsite was a reminder of lost love.

Thousands of pilgrims had arrived in Mecca for the hajj. And the Kaaba was not Mecca's only attraction. Once the pilgrims had fed their spirits with prayer, most of them went on to the Ukaz fair, to feed other appetites.

The fair was held on the edge of town. I had never seen anything like it. Mystics called fakirs whirled and walked on burning coals. Hawkers called out the benefits of their wares: potions that would make men strong and women beautiful, bone or feather amulets for good luck, and coils of colorful yarn to weave into sturdy cloth. An African snake handler swung a cobra in the air. A monkey danced to the jangling beat of a tambourine. Soothsayers hunched over the palms of their customers. Men reeled among the attractions, drunk on date palm wine or a foul-smelling brew made from mare's milk. The sharp, cloying smell of animals, spices, and too many people pressing together under the hot sun hung in the air.

The poetry contest was one of the fair's biggest attractions. I tried to forget about the activity around me and think of nothing but my poem. I desperately wanted my name inscribed in the Kaaba. It would bring honor to myself and to Zayed— and to Omar, as my teacher. Best of all, I would use the prize of a sack of silver to buy my own camel and join a caravan, and leave Mecca's walls behind. My throat ached from practicing. I sucked on sweets made of honey and swallowed some asafetida— horrible, bitter stuff, but it kept my throat soothed.

Finally, it was time for the competition. I took my place in a row of a dozen men and boys seated on stools on a stage. The contest had drawn an eager crowd, ready to cheer for their favorite. I could see that Zayed had been able to get away from his work. He waved and gave me a big smile.

I listened to the others recite, licking my dry lips. One poet must have tried to calm his nerves with date wine, because when it was his turn he shouted out the first line of his poem and promptly lost his place. He began again, but again he forgot the words. The crowd jeered. Red-faced, he left the stage. Someone removed his empty stool.

Somebody prodded me. With a start, I realized it was my turn. I stood as tall as I could. I closed my eyes for a moment and willed myself back in the desert. I thought about my father's sweet voice and began to recite, letting the familiar words flow from me.

In the crowd, Zayed was applauding and whistling and calling out my name, trying to get the audience on my side. Then he ducked into the crowd, bobbed up in a different spot, and cheered for me all over again.

I didn't let him break my concentration on the difficult rhythms of the verse. I let the poem carry me, and I was nearing the end when I saw a man in the crowd throw his arms around Zayed.

"Zayed, is it really you? Thanks be to all the gods, you are alive!"

I recognized him. It was Ali, my father's cousin. He must have arrived for the hajj.

I realized I didn't know where I was in the poem. Had I said this verse already? I stumbled on, trying to speak and to listen at the same time.

Ali's joy lasted only a moment. "We thought you were dead, Cousin. Aye, aye, here you are enjoying yourself at a fair when you have yet to avenge your father's death. How can this be? You are a disgrace."

I was glad he didn't recognize me—probably because I'd grown almost as tall as Zayed in the months we'd been in Mecca. Others turned to stare, and some of them yelled at him to hush. But Ali went on, spraying Zayed with spittle as he ranted.

"You are a worthless nothing! A No Name! You are no longer a member of our clan."

Zayed had had enough. He shouted, "I belong to the household of Abu l'Hakam now, and he is the most important man in all of Arabia!" He pulled away from Ali and elbowed through the crowd, jostling spectators, who cursed him as he passed.

Desperately, I fumbled for the words, but I couldn't remember what came next. I made up something, just to end the poem, and went back to my spot, wishing I were invisible. I was out of the competition.

For the first time in years, Omar had not taken part in the contest. Instead, he had been enjoying the fair, joining the audience only when it was my turn. When he found me sitting glumly among the other losers in the shade beside the tent, he didn't look well himself.

"Sorry, boy, must be something I ate." He burped. "Ah, don't worry about the contest. You did well until the very end. Next year you will win! Have you had a chance to see much of the fair? I suppose not. Why don't you take a walk around?"

I was in no mood to see the sights. I wanted to talk to Zayed, but he had disappeared. I needed to find some peace of mind, so I went to the Kaaba. Something about that holy place always calmed me. But when I got there, men were milling around the door and there was a lot of loud talk. I pushed through the crowd until I was close enough to see that someone had nailed a piece of sheepskin to the door of the building. A man read it aloud in a booming voice. It said that nobody was supposed to have anything to do with anybody who was a Hashimite. Nobody could buy from or sell to a Hashimite. If they met one in the street, they had to turn their back. This was an official order, and anybody found disobeying it would do so under pain of punishment.

I thought about the good Hashimite men I knew, Walid and Omar and, of course, Muhammad. What was going to happen to them now?

I didn't want to go back to the fair, so I made my way through the streets clogged with pilgrims to Omar's stall. Even before I got there, I knew something was very wrong. I found Omar bent over, picking at a pile of his belongings. He kept very little in the stall: the carpet I slept on, a bench, a small stool, a table he used for writing. All that was left was a smoldering mess.

I was horrified. "What happened? Did I leave a lantern lit last night?"

"No, no, I was warned that something like this would happen. It's because I'm a Companion. The Companions are targets for the Quraysh. I'm only surprised they waited this long."

"Don't worry, Omar, we'll set up the stall again."

"No, it's no use, Fallah. Yesterday, somebody threw rotten oranges at my wife. And there have been other incidents I haven't told you about. One of our friends borrowed a large sum of money last month from a wealthy Quraysh merchant to make some purchases for his business. It was agreed he would have a year to repay it, but last week the merchant came and demanded the money back immediately. When he couldn't pay, my friend lost his business and left Mecca. Another one of our Companions was falsely accused of theft, and now he will be tried for a crime he didn't commit. What are the chances he will go free when the case will be decided by a judge from the Quraysh clan? No, Fallah, this has been brewing for quite some time, and it will only get worse."

I told him about the warning posted at the Kaaba.

"This place will never be safe for us while the Quraysh are in power. They know that Muhammad cares about his followers, and they hope to stifle him by threatening us. Muhammad has said we should leave Mecca and go to Medina, to protect ourselves. I hate to leave, but the time has come. Fallah, you are most welcome to come with us."

I thought about it. I could not leave without Zayed, and I knew that Zayed would not leave with the Companions. The way he saw it, Muhammad was just a troublemaker. He believed that the Quraysh would always be in power because they always *had* been in power. He was determined to throw his lot in with Abu l'Hakam and his powerful tribe.

Omar took my silence as an answer.

"I understand. But this is a world in which you need more than a head full of poems. May Allah be with you."

Omar's stall was mine now. I rebuilt it and laid new palm leaves over it so that I could sit in the shade while I recited. One by one, people returned to hear me. And in the evenings, I would sometimes gather with the Companions to hear what Muhammad was teaching.

One day, a lady who often came to listen was reduced to tears by a poem I recited. She pressed a gold ring into my palm as payment. I protested, but she closed her hand around mine and said her lost son had loved words and he would have loved a poet to have his ring.

That same afternoon, I had just begun a poem Omar had taught me when a shadow fell across me. I looked up to see a well-dressed, burly man snarling at me. "Thief! You have stolen my son's ring!"

I knew it was no use to argue, so I quickly slipped the ring off my finger and held it out to him. I tried to apologize, but he would have none of it.

"You are the pup who worked with the troublemaker Omar. You were seen consorting with Muhammad." He spat on the ground as he said the name.

After that, everything happened as quickly as a flash flood. The owner of the ring was a head man among the Quraysh. Two younger men—probably his personal guards—grabbed me.

"This boy is a dirty thief!" the man shouted. "This is the kind of scum that the liar Muhammad befriends and calls brother. What are things coming to in this city?"

He had me arrested and thrown into a jail cell.

For three days I sat in this cell that was little better than an animal's cage, with no food and only the occasional cup of water. I had no idea whether Zayed even knew what had happened to me, or if he did know but had decided I brought this trouble upon myself. Could he really have turned his back on me that way?

When I was brought to trial, I held out no hope. I remembered what Omar had said about the chances of any friend of Muhammad's getting justice from the Quraysh. I was right. It was no coincidence that I had been given that ring only to be accused of stealing it the very same day. This Quraysh head man had set me up so that they could be rid of another friend of Muhammad's. I was sentenced to be buried up to my neck in the sand, in the heat of the day. It would not take long for me to die. That, at least, was a blessing.

Now I was chained inside a small, airless stone building, waiting to be executed. Again I was alone, with only my thoughts and my poems to keep me company. And then, the night before the sentence was to be carried out, I heard a voice calling my name. It was Zayed! He pressed his mouth to the narrow slit that was the only window.

"Fallah, I told you to stay away from the Companions. They have brought you nothing but suffering."

"Help me, Brother." The building was like an oven and my mouth was parched. It hurt to speak.

Zayed started to cry. "I don't know what to do. When I heard what happened, I went straight to Abu l'Hakam to beg that you be forgiven. Fallah, I tried. I tried desperately. I lay flat on the ground at Abu l'Hakam's feet. He didn't even know who I was. He said, 'You and your brother are nothing to me. Why, any one of my cats means more to me.' He told me to get out of his sight, and never to let him lay eyes on me again."

"I know you tried," I whispered.

"Then I remembered our father's cousin, Ali. There was a chance that he was still in Mecca. It was like finding a single grain of sand, but I knew that, as a bedouin, he would be drawn to the poets near the Kaaba. That's where I started to look, and sure enough, that's where he was. I tried to kiss his hand, but he pulled it away as if it were on fire. I won't tell you what he said, but we can't look for help there."

I was in despair. Through my tears, I said my goodbyes to Zayed.

I didn't know that a person could feel so alone. I passed that night making up a poem. Perhaps what Muhammad said was true, and life after death would be more just than the life I'd known and the death I was about to suffer. I sang the verses with a cracked, dry voice. If these were to be my last words, they would be about Allah. All the gods and the jinn had vanished for me. I gave myself to Allah.

At dawn, I was dragged out of the building. Someone had already dug a pit and I was thrown into it. One man held me while two others filled the pit around me with sand so that only my shoulders and head appeared aboveground. The sand pressed in on me painfully. Worse, as the sun rose, the sand heated up. I was in agony, suffocating from the pressure of the baking sand and desperate for water. The Quraysh who had accused me stood and watched, waiting for me to die.

My eyes became so dry and cloudy that I hardly recognized Zayed. He had a water skin in his hands, but when he tried to come near me, somebody held him back. I didn't know how much longer I could stand it. The sand was burning my body and the sun was scorching my face and head.

And that is when the miracle occurred. At least, it was a miracle to me—the heat made me so dizzy that I can't remember everything. I saw the outline of a man talking to my accuser. I couldn't see who he was or hear what he said. I must have fainted, because the next thing I knew, I was being carried into a house and given cool water. Zayed sat beside me, holding a wet cloth to my forehead.

When I revived a bit, I asked Zayed what had happened. He had a hard time speaking through his tears.

"After I left you last night, I thought it was over for you. The only thing I could do was come here and wait until they brought you out. I wasn't going to let you die alone. Or worse, with no one but that demon who had you arrested to gloat over you. I wanted to kill him."

"Why did they let me go? Did that Quraysh feel bad for torturing me?"

"No such thing! All that wicked man cared about was money. You won't believe this. You fainted, and I thought, 'At least he's no longer in pain.' Then a man appeared. I could hear him offering money to the Quraysh to buy you."

"Buy me? Am I a slave?" I tried to sit up.

Zayed took me by the shoulders. I screamed when he touched my sunburned skin.

"I'm so sorry! No, don't worry. As soon as this man bought you and made sure you were safe, he set you free. And guess who it was? It was Walid, the merchant."

Walid stepped out of a shadowy corner. "Word spreads quickly among the Companions. You were being punished because they believed you were one of us. I didn't know we had met before until I saw your brother."

As he spoke, I realized that, with my whole heart, I was ready to be a Companion. It wasn't just gratitude for being saved—it was knowing that there were people who believed in justice and what was right, people who didn't care that I had no possessions and no father and no tribe. I belonged with them.

Zayed hung his head. "Walid, I have something to tell you. There is a plot to murder Muhammad."

I was furious. "A plot? How long have you known? We have to warn him!" I struggled to sit up again.

Walid took my hand. "Do you think such a plot could be kept quiet? In Mecca, where everyone knows everyone else? Don't worry, Muhammad is safe, Allah be praised. He left Mecca on a camel in the dark. The Quraysh sent out search parties, of course, but Muhammad and his companion, Abu Bakr, had a plan. They knew that the Quraysh would think they'd gone north, so instead they rode south. A shepherd covered their tracks with his flock of sheep. When they felt it was safe, Muhammad and Abu Bakr swung north and rode on to Medina. My household will follow tomorrow." Walid paused, and looked at me with kindness. "Will you travel with us? Think about it." Walid rested his hand on Zayed's head for a moment and left us alone together.

When he was gone, I took Zayed's hand. "You know where my heart lies, Brother, but I will not go without you."

"Fallah, I know there's nothing here for us anymore. Nobody

would dare to listen to you recite, and as for me, well, I thought that if I was a loyal servant, Abu l'Hakam would take care of me." He snorted. "And yet to leave behind everything we've ever known, the ways of our grandfathers, the gods, the spirits . . . It's such a hard thing to ask."

I searched desperately for the words that would convince him.

"What roads are open to us? We can't go back to our family. You would have to commit a murder, and eventually so would I, because I would have to avenge *your* death. And you've seen that we can't rely on the Quraysh. To them we're just nameless orphans who count for nothing. This is our chance to be gathered in. Allah will give us strength. We can be part of a new kind of family, where it won't matter that we are poor and fatherless. As long as we dedicate ourselves to doing good in this world, we can stand proudly in it."

As I spoke, I felt the way I did whenever I was caught up in the spell of a great poem. The words were no longer mine alone. In them I heard the echo of my father's voice, who had passed on the gift of poetry to me, and my mother's, who had bravely sent us away to save us, and Muhammad's, as he spoke to the Companions about the way to live a righteous life.

"Zayed, if we go to Medina, we will take our place among the family of believers. This is a great gift we've been offered."

I waited for Zayed to speak. Finally, he squeezed my hand. "I have heard you, little brother. So it shall be."

When we called Walid back in, we thanked him. It was Zayed who said, "We will go to Medina. And we'll care for your camels along the way."

For the first time that day, I saw Walid smile.

As we left Mecca behind for the long journey north, I felt as if I had emerged from a dark cave where stone walls had surrounded me, blocking out the light. I realized how I had longed for pure air, for the ceaseless sighing wind, and the vast open space. Most of all, I had missed the beauty of the endless, starry night sky.

EPILOGUE

Like wasps whose nest has been disturbed, the Quraysh grew angrier once Muhammad left Mecca. They rallied an army to attack him in Medina. Battle after battle left many dead. Finally, a peace treaty was signed by the Quraysh. There was to be no war, no treachery, and the Prophet could return to Mecca.

This was not yet the end. When Muhammad returned to Mecca, the Quraysh didn't want to be known for having broken the treaty, but they weren't about to forgive Muhammad, either. Instead, they supplied his enemies with weapons.

Muhammad knew he'd have to take Mecca, but he wanted no violence, so he devised a plan. He ordered his men to spread out around the city, and they were each told to light a fire. Seeing that many campfires, the people of Mecca would naturally assume that a vast army was surrounding the city. And that is what happened. Without shedding any blood, the Prophet had won a great victory.

When Muhammad spoke for the last time, a crowd of thousands stood in brutal heat to hear about Allah and to pray. Muhammad spoke to them, saying, "You will be asked about me, so what will you say?" Together they answered: "We bear witness that you have conveyed Allah's message and have performed your duty and that you have meant goodness to us."

NOTES

MOSES

When did Moses Live?

Moses' birth is recorded as taking place 2,368 years before the Common Era, or almost 5,000 years ago.

Hebrew

Hebrew is a word that was first used in reference to Abraham, describing all his descendants. *Hebrew* is still an important word because it is also the name of the language of Jewish prayer and the language used in the State of Israel.

Another word that describes the same people is *Israelite*. Abraham's grandson Jacob is given the name Israel in the Torah, and that is the name by which the people are known in the Bible.

Israeli has remained the name of the people in Hebrew and in other languages.

The people of Israel were divided into twelve tribes. One was the tribe of Judah, and that may be the source of the word *Jew*. *Judah* was also the name of the territory of which Jerusalem was the capital, and which Jews in ancient times looked to as their homeland.

But all three terms, *Hebrew*, *Israelite*, and *Jew*, refer to the same people—people who are descendants of Abraham, who was chosen to declare that there is only one God.

The Holy Text of the Jewish People

The holy text of the Jewish people is called the Torah, a word that comes from the Hebrew word meaning "instruction." It is made up of the Five Books of Moses. The first is Genesis, which describes the creation of the world. Exodus is the second book, and it recounts how the Hebrews left slavery in Egypt. The third book is Leviticus, and it is mostly about priestly matters such as sacrifices. Numbers, the fourth book, is about the wandering of the people in the wilderness before they came to the Promised Land. And Deuteronomy tells about the death of Moses just before the people entered the Promised Land.

The words of the Torah are written by hand on scrolls wound around two wooden poles. The scribes who do the writing must be very skillful because a Torah scroll cannot contain any mistakes.

The Ten Commandments

Along with the belief in one God, the Ten Commandments are sometimes described as the Torah's greatest contribution to civilization. They are said to have been given to Moses on Mount Sinai when he was leading the Hebrews out of Egypt to the land of Canaan, where they could have a permanent home. The Ten Commandments are:

I am the Lord your God.

You shall worship no other gods besides Me.

You shall not carry God's name in vain.

Remember the Sabbath day to make it holy.

Honor your father and mother.

You shall not murder.

You shall not commit adultery.

You shall not steal.

You shall not bear false witness against your neighbor.

You shall not covet anything that belongs to your neighbor.

The Government of Egypt

The Egyptian Empire began 4,000 years before the Common Era, or about 6,000 years ago, and it lasted for about 4,500 years. Everything in Egypt was owned by the Pharaoh, including every stone, plant, animal, and person. The Pharaoh's power came from the belief that he or she was not just a human leader, but a god. The Pharaoh always had a great many advisers, mostly priests. Below the priests were all kinds of government officials. Egypt was divided into provinces and each province had its own governor. The officials made sure that taxes were collected, buildings were built, and the army was always at the ready.

There was no currency in Egypt at the time, so everybody paid their taxes in work. Most people lived on farms near the fertile Nile valley. They had no say at all in the way their country was run.

Weaving

Weaving is one of the world's oldest arts. A scrap of woven material found in Faiyûm has been estimated to be around 7,000 years old. Egyptians most commonly wove flax into linen cloth, though they also could weave wool. In the earliest times, two weavers—usually children or slaves—worked a loom together.

The Seder

Passover, the holiday that commemorates Moses leading the Hebrews out of slavery, has been celebrated by Jews around the world for thousands of years. It begins with a ritual meal called the seder, meaning "order," with, discussion, songs, special foods, and prayers to tell the story of the exodus from Egypt. The people taking part in the seder use a book called a Haggadah, which means "telling." The Haggadah brings together biblical quotes, commentaries, and explanations about why specific foods are eaten at the meal. The seder is meant to remind the participants that they were once slaves and are now obliged to work so that nobody is downtrodden anymore.

JESUS

Marking Time

For about 1,500 years, people have been using the labels BC and AD to refer to a specific year. BC means "before Christ," but it is now often written as BCE, for "before Common Era." We now frequently use CE, meaning "Common Era," in place of AD, "in the year of our Lord," or *Anno Domini* in Latin. We don't have a year that's zero. In this system, Jesus was born in the year 1 AD. The year before that is 1 BC, and the year before that is 2 BC. Although it is now an almost worldwide way of marking time, some countries did not use BC and AD until the last century.

When did Christianity begin?

Right after Jesus died, when he was thirty-three years old, his message began to be carried far and wide by his disciples. They did so with great courage, because they were often cruelly persecuted for their beliefs. The Roman emperor even blamed them for a great fire that almost destroyed the city of Rome. Armenia is considered to have been the first Christian country, having accepted Christianity in the year 301. Ten years later, the Roman emperor Constantine the First issued what was called an Edict of Toleration, ending the persecution of Christians. Then, on February 27 in the year 380, the emperor Theodosius passed a law making Christianity the official Church of Rome.

Why is this belief called Christianity?

The word *Christianity* comes from the name Jesus Christ. *Jesus* is the Greek form of the Hebrew name Joshua. The word *Christ* is the Greek version of the Hebrew word *Moshiach*, or Messiah. And Messiah means "the anointed one."

The Holy Text of the Christian People

The Bible is the collection of texts that are the sacred foundation of both Judaism and Christianity, and the part of the Bible that focuses on Jesus' life and teachings is often called the New Testament.

For most Christians, the Bible includes the works that make up the Jewish Torah (which Christians refer to as the Old Testament) as well as the New Testament. (Jews don't consider the Torah to be the Old Testament; for Jews it is simply the Bible.)

The Bible is made up of "books," though they aren't books as we know them. Instead, they are writings that were originally recorded on scrolls and subsequently brought together to form a unified sacred text. The New Testament is made up of the

Gospels of Matthew, Mark, Luke, and John; the Acts of the Apostles; the letters, or epistles, of Paul, named according to their recipients (the Romans, the Corinthians, and so on); the Catholic epistles written by James, Peter, John, and Jude; and finally the Apocalypse, the Revelation of Saint John.

Bibles are available in just about every language, including American Sign Language. Nobody knows how many are in print, but a conservative guess is two billion.

The Disciples

The twelve men selected by Jesus from among his followers to spread his message are called the disciples, or apostles. They were the men closest to Jesus during the time that he preached. Not everybody agrees about exactly which of the followers became apostles, but the list likely includes Peter, Andrew, James, John, Philip, Bartholomew, Thomas, Matthew, James the Less, Jude, and Simon. The twelfth was the traitor Judas Iscariot.

After Jesus died, the apostles went their separate ways, spreading his teachings. Peter and his brother Andrew had both been fishermen. According to Christian tradition, after the Crucifixion, Peter went to Rome and founded the Roman Catholic Church. James was beheaded by the Romans because of his teaching. John is believed to be the author of the Gospel of John as well as the last book in the Bible, the Book of Revelation. Philip came from modern-day Jordan. Bartholomew may have been a friend of Philip's; he was from Cana in Galilee. The New Testament doesn't tell us anything about Thomas before he met Jesus, but some people believe he carried Jesus' teachings to Syria, Persia, and finally India. We also know little about Simon. Matthew was a tax collector for the Romans before Jesus met him in Capernaum and invited him to become one of his followers. He may have gone to Ethiopia to spread Jesus' message. The second James is sometimes called "the Less," not because he wasn't important but to distinguish him from the other James. According to tradition, Jude preached in Judea, Samaria, Syria, and Libya.

The Christian Church's Most Holy Day

The oldest and most important holy day of the Christian Church is Easter. Christians believe that when he was crucified, Jesus Christ died for the sins of the world, and by being resurrected, he gave hope of everlasting life for believers.

Many Christians observe Easter on the first Sunday after the first full moon following the vernal equinox, which takes place on March 21. In other words, it falls somewhere between March 22 and April 25. In the Orthodox Churches, Easter coincides with the Jewish Passover. In fact, in many languages the name is Pasch, from the Hebrew *Pesach*, or Passover. In English, the name Easter may come from the Germanic goddess of spring, Eostre.

MUHAMMAD

Poetry in Arabia

Poets and poetry were much admired in ancient Arabia. Poets were considered to be a combination of historian, fortune-teller, and commentator. Their poems were about all kinds of subjects, some more serious than others. There were poems that praised specific tribes and made fun of others. Many poems had a sense of longing for a lost time, a lost place, or a lost love. The *sha'ir* wrote poems and often had an apprentice called a *rawi*, who recited. Recitation required extraordinary feats of memorization.

Around a hundred years after Muhammad's death, the best poems, called "the hung poems" because they were hung on the wall or the door of the Kaaba, were collected into one document, containing a single poem from each of seven famous poets.

Ramadan

Ramadan is the ninth month of the Islamic calendar, and Muslims consider it the holiest time of the year. Muslims observe

Ramadan by acts of charity, prayer, and fasting from sunrise to sunset. Putting aside a time for reflection has roots that go back thousands of years, when people in Arabia would retreat from daily life to meditate and to pray.

Observing Ramadan is one of the Five Pillars of Faith for Muslims. The others are: faith in the Creator of the Universe, prayer five times a day, acts of charity, and pilgrimage to Mecca.

The Holy Text of the Muslim People

The words of the Quran, the Muslim people's religious text, are believed to have been revealed to Muhammad by the angel Jibril, or Gabriel. Verse by verse, Muhammad memorized the revelations as they poured from him, and he shared them with others. Those people memorized them too, and some of them wrote them down on stone tablets or pieces of parchment. Not long after Muhammad died, in 632 CE, Abu Bakr wanted to bring together all the verses in one written text. Scribes collected the verses from written records and from the memories of those who had learned them by heart. Twenty years after Muhammad's death there was a complete, written Quran.

Camels

Because of the lack of water and the extreme heat, the Arabian Peninsula was one of the world's hardest places to live. It would have been almost impossible were it not for camels. Their ability to carry heavy loads, to run as fast as horses, and to go without food and water for long periods of time made these beasts an essential part of desert life from the time they were first domesticated, between four thousand and two thousand years ago.

Camels are wonderfully suited for the desert. An inner eyelid and long eyelashes protect the camel's eyes against sand. The camel's nostrils can close, which is useful in a sandstorm. Wide feet make it possible to walk over shifting sand. The humps (one for Arabian dromedary camels and two for the much rarer Bactrian camels) store fat that gives the animal strength and endurance. When there's little food, the camel lives off the fat in its hump. It can go for months without eating and a week without drinking. But when it does drink, it can gulp down 32 gallons (145 liters) of water in less than half an hour.

ACKNOWLEDGMENTS

This book would not have been possible without the help of several generous and knowledgeable people. Professor Don Akenson, author of *Surpassing Wonder: The Invention of the Bible and the Talmuds*, was of immense help. Rabbi Tina Grimberg of Congregation Darchei Noam in Toronto inspired the character of Dina, and extraordinary Egyptologist Gayle Gibson brought the House of Weavers to life for me. I learned a great deal about Muhammad from Raheel Razal, President, Council for Muslims Facing Tomorrow, and about the bedouins and their wonderful poetry from Elizabeth Key Fowden. I am also grateful to Fred Unwalla, editor in chief at the Pontifical Institute of Mediaeval Studies, for helping me make connections and for acting as a wise sounding board. Anything I got right is thanks to their answering my many questions. The mistakes are mine and mine alone.

To everyone at Annick Press, I can't thank you enough for entrusting me with this idea and for making this book possible, and to Kong Njo and Sheryl Shapiro for making it beautiful. And finally, to Catherine Marjoribanks, who tackled the frustrating job of editing an editor: thank you for your unfailingly good advice.